Everything That We've Buried

AND OTHER STORIES

CLEMSON

LITERATURE SERIES

CONVERSE

KYLER S. CAMPBELL

Everything That We've Buried

AND OTHER STORIES

ISBN 978-1-63804-227-3

Published by Clemson University Press.
Visit our website to learn more about our publishing program:
www.clemson.edu/press.

Typeset by Kyrsten Shealy
Cover by Mars O'Keefe
Cover image created by Ana Harris

Contents

Acknowledgements

"How Will They Remember You" first appeared in the Fall 2023 issue of *Cumberland River Review*

"Caretta Caretta" first appeared in the 2014 issue of *Driftwood*

"Everything That We've Buried" first appeared in the Fall 2017 issue of *Longshot Island.*

"Zombie Jesus" first appeared in the Fall 2023 issue of *Flash Fiction Magazine.*

"Smoke on the Wind" first appeared in the 2017 issue of *Sheepshead Review.*

"Tongues of Fire" first appeared in 2014 in *Paradise Review*

How Will They Remember You?

He stepped through the trees like a man outside of time. Alcide Fonteneau brushed the leaves and dirt from his hair and beard, blinking steadily in the afternoon light. The Louisiana sun burned bright in a cloudless sky, lighting up open fields and clearings that seemed to go on forever in every direction. The soles of his shoes had worn through days before, and the last meal he remembered was small by even the poorest standard. But he was home now. And for the first time since he'd left to fight the war between the states, he remembered what hope felt like.

He thought of his wife, Rachel, and their farm, the small patch of land his family had cleared and tilled and cultivated for generations. She would be waiting for him at their home. He had pictured their reunion hundreds of times on the journey home, but he never held it too tightly. He knew the danger of letting a dream become an expectation, and so he set them all aside

Alcide pulled on his coat, the Confederate insignia hanging limp and threadbare. The lapel was stained with old blood, most of which had browned over the time it took him to get to this spot. The oldest stains were his blood. But the recent patches, the ones that still gave off a faint metallic smell, belonged to his son. In the high morning sunshine though, no one passing by could tell the difference.

The tide of war had come in like a midnight thunderstorm, settling over his small corner of the world. Men had been swept up in dreams of honor and glory, the chance to be remembered as heroes of the "War Between the States." Everywhere Alcide went, the men's hearts burned for violence and glory, and the women caught their breath at the thought of a well-pressed uniform while fighting the fear of life as a widow or a grieving mother.

When that tide of duty to God and their new Confederacy reached their corner of Louisiana, Alcide, and other reluctant recruits, were faced with enlistment or treason. And so he reluctantly joined the effort. But when he dressed in that iron gray Confederate coat for the first time, he was not alone. His only son, sixteen-year-old Joaquin, stood next to him, showing off his own iron gray uniform, beaming with the courage of ignorance and youth.

Rachel, Alcide's wife, pleaded to him, "You take care of him, Alcide Fonteneau. He's yours to protect." She had often referred to Joaquin as "her heart" and "her dream" since he was the only one of their children to live past infancy. Joaquin's life was so precious to them both that they never felt a need to test God by trying for another. And though he would not admit it, Alcide did not think he would survive burying another child.

Their first child's name was Emmaline, after Alcide's grandmother. And when the baby died, he and Rachel wept for days. But each new pregnancy brought new sorrow and a new grave marker under the oak tree behind their home. And so, when Rachel became pregnant with Joaquin, they refused to name him for the first six months of his life until they knew the boy would survive. As he grew and thrived on their farm, Alcide and Rachel believed their lives were complete. Alcide even found himself forgetting about the other children buried under the oak tree. As Joaquin grew into a healthy young man, the memory of their other children began to scab over until each one was just a faint scar in his mind.

And so, as war swept Alcide and his only son away from their home, Alcide prayed for Joaquin, asking an estranged God for protection as they marched out past the lines of St. Landry Parish.

All that, the marching and the tide of war, was just an echo now, useless memory that wouldn't serve him in rebuilding his life. But the town had changed since he'd left. As he walked the roads leading in and out of Opelousas, Alcide saw faces that he once knew, old men who had gotten older and boys now on the edge of manhood. Any young and able men had been called to defend the cause, leaving the leftovers to look after the home front.

A smooth-faced boy carrying a sack of beans passed by Alcide with a polite but concerned greeting, noting the insignia on his coat. Across the street, Women, busy clearing dust out of their houses, stopped their sweeping to stare at this new stranger, then led their children inside.

Alcide stopped at a store just outside of town, grateful for a relief from the afternoon heat. The chatter inside fell to whispers. The clerk drooped his tired old body across the counter and, with whatever strength he'd once had, waved to Alcide.

"What can we help you with, stranger?" The man asked.

"Just passing through," Alcide said with as much kindness as was left in him.

"That's a heavy coat for this time of year," the clerk said, pointing at Alcide's jacket.

Alcide could feel the cool wood floor through the holes in his boots.

"Unique, I'd say," the man continued.

"I don't want any trouble, sir."

The man gestured to the blood stains on his lapel.

"Looks like you already found it."

"It's old. From the war," Alcide said.

The man did his best to smile. "Most folks would rather just move on," he said. "They don't need relics hanging about, reminding them of what it's like to lose everything."

The store had gone silent. Every woman and child and old gray beard stared at Alcide. He wiped his hands on his tattered pants and wished the clerk a good day. Outside, the sun had only just started to descend from its high place in the sky. He pulled his coat tight and headed down the road that would lead him back home to Rachel.

~

The march to war was endless. Soon, Alcide and Joaquin lost track of the days. Once their company crossed the state line into Arkansas, rumors spread that they were heading towards a large group of Union soldiers. And as that violent reality began to settle into their minds, more and more men deserted camp during the night. Every morning, the company awoke to find another tent empty and abandoned.

One night, in the dark of their tent, Alcide asked his son, "How do you want to be remembered?"

Joaquin considered the question. Finally, he said, "I want to be remembered as a great soldier."

Alcide knew these as the dreams of youth, the dreams of the ignorant and prideful who didn't know what it was to hold the power of life and death in their hands. *He wants to be remembered for courage,* Alcide thought. *But we will both carry a legacy of violence.*

Alcide's own father was a man with violence in his heart and the skills to see it done. As a child, he had watched his father sling a rifle across his back and rush out to meet his neighbor at their property line. No one could say who shot first, but everyone knew why it happened. The two men had killed each other over three feet of land, a border dispute that claimed their lives and marked their families' legacies forever. That night, Alcide had hitched his father's corpse to a sled, lashed together from branches and twine, listening to the buzzards circling patiently above them.

"What about you?" Joaquin asked his father.

Alcide's memories evaporated, and he turned to see the dark outline of his son, lying next to him.

"I want to be remembered as your father," he said and rolled over to sleep.

As he drifted off that night, Alcide tried to remember his father as a kind man, a good man, a caring father. But in his mind, he only saw those buzzards circling all the way up to eternity and the twisted expression of hatred forever carved into his father's face.

Off in the distance, gunfire popped, sparse at first but soon one after another. He wasn't sure how long he'd been asleep, maybe hours, maybe minutes. Soon shouting began to break through the summer night. The news came fast and loud: blue coats had marched through the night and encircled their camp. "Fight for your lives," the shouts said. "Fight for your families."

Alcide shook his son awake and began gathering their boots and clothes.

"We're leaving," he said.

Joaquin came to and said, "I'm going to help them fight,"

"You're going to do what I tell you." Alcide turned his coat inside out and checked for any identifying insignias.

"I ain't no deserter," Joaquin said and made to grab his rifle and join the skirmish.

Outside their tent, men's dying screams came rolling in waves. Alcide grabbed his son by the neck and took the gun from his hand. Then he threw his son to the ground. "We are leaving here together," he said.

He watched as the bravado disappeared from Joaquin's eyes like a gun powder flash. Alcide reached out and helped Joaquin up of the ground. The two tossed a few essentials into their packs and made for the edge of camp.

When they had made it past the worst fighting unnoticed, Alcide allowed himself to feel hope again. He would see Rachel again. They would both see Joaquin grow strong and wise, and their son would lay them to rest of their children under the oak tree behind their home.

Alcide turned around to see the smoke rising from the camp, and, in a flash, a rifle stock met his temple. He collapsed under a clear night sky, lying next to his only son. His last thought was not of Joaquin, but of his other children and their grave markers under the giant oak tree.

As he slipped out of consciousness, Alcide wondered if he would see those children again. He wanted to hold them and carry them like he had Joaquin. Somewhere behind him, a chorus of men's screams carried on a cool nighttime breeze.

~

He made his way out of town, feeling every footstep through the sores on his feet. Everywhere he went people stopped their tasks or hushed their conversations. They watched him, and only when they knew they were out of his reach would they whisper about his disheveled state or scowl at his coat and the memories it conjured for them.

A few miles from town, he found himself standing outside his home again, and Alcide's hope was renewed. But the house was not how Alcide remembered it. The boards on the outside were either weathered or broken, holding only the distant memory of paint. The front porch sagged into the dirt, and most of the windows were clouded over with dust and growth. Out back, the soy and corn crops wilted and rotted. For the first time in what felt like a lifetime, Alcide took off his coat, folding it neatly in the crook of his arm.

The door to the house cracked open and a woman stared at him. He knew his wife, Rachel. Despite the age in her face and her gaunt frame, he knew this was Rachel. The dark curtain of hair had thinned and greyed, but her eyes still gleamed green in the sunlight like he remembered.

Rachel sighed, as if he'd been late for dinner and hadn't sent word. Alcide stood straight, making himself slightly more presentable.

"Come in," she finally said.

Alcide, like a dutiful soldier, followed her orders and stepped into the house he had once known.

Unlike the outside, the inside was nearly unchanged. Each piece of furniture was in its proper place and the old floors still held their dull gleam. Rachel sat across from him at their table. He wondered if she was still, indeed, his wife. Both of them waited for the other one to speak, knowing that it would begin a conversation that neither wanted to have. Rachel had always been fluent in silence, accustomed to holding her words close. Alcide was not, and he broke the space between them.

"You're still here," Alcide said finally.

"So are you," his wife replied. She stared at his coat. "You might want to lose that."

Alcide draped the coat on the chair next to him as if saving a seat for visitor.

"It's all I've got left," he said.

Rachel wore a small gold band on her finger, one that Alcide had never seen before.

"Lot of people changed their mind about the war," she said.

He thought about the shop owner from earlier. "Maybe we need to be reminded," he said. "Maybe it's worse to forget."

Rachel shook her head. "We were all different folks back then," she said.

He stared at her ring again. "You re-married," he said.

She let the silence speak on her behalf.

Alcide's chest sunk, and his head began to swim. "I can forgive you for that," he said without really hearing himself.

"I don't need your forgiveness," she snapped.

Alcide wanted to know more about this man, who he was and was he good to his wife. But those questions seemed so far away now, too far for him to reach.

"I thought you were dead," Rachel said.

"I might as well have been."

Rachel sat quiet for a moment, then asked "Where is our son?"

He dragged his ragged fingernails across the unfinished wood of the kitchen table. Behind him, a metal pot began to boil on the wood burning stove, sizzling and whistling through the silence.

~

Though they had survived the ambush, Alcide and Joaquin, along with a quarter of their company, were taken to a prison camp somewhere north of Tennessee. Every day, as they marched north through the hills, a new batch of men died from exhaustion or illness or cruelty. They considered the dead to be lucky. Alcide and the others had lived their entire lives plowing lowlands or skimming through bayous. Their blood was too thin and their lungs too weak for the mountainous terrain. Alcide watched his son's once sturdy legs shrivel and his own shoulders become small and fragile like a child's. He could feel his bones rising to the surface of his skin, stretched thin across his frame.

When they finally reached the prison camp, Alcide stared at the mountains that surrounded them on all sides. He'd never seen anything so big in his life. Had he been in a different circumstance, he might have enjoyed them. But over time, they began to feel like a fence, keeping him here in this place while time passed by without him beyond their walls.

One night, as small camp fires dotted the grounds of the prison camp, Alcide, Joaquin, and a few other prisoners sat huddled together, cooking their rations or whatever rodent they had happened to catch that day. One of the men finally spoke up.

"We're going to escape here," he said.

Some men were silent and some straightened their backs at this news.

Alcide listened to the young men make plans to escape, each one more stupid than the last. As the firelight flickered, Alcide could see his son Joaquin becoming entranced with the idea. That fire of violence rekindled behind his eyes.

Out of their small collection, twenty men had conspired to overrun the night shift guards and climb the wooden walls and disappear into the night. When Alcide tried to interject, the men had shouted him down, so he left it alone.

"I don't want you to go," Alcide told his son the night before their planned escape.

"We can't stay here."

"You can't fight the guards," Alcide said.

"Is this how you want to be remembered?" Joaquin asked his father. "As a prisoner?"

For a moment, Alcide imagined asking his own father that same question. But in his imagination, his father, loading his rifle with precision and poise, said nothing.

Alcide said to his son, "I want to be remembered for keeping you safe."

They lay together as the rain loosened the ground beneath their tent, the new mud cooling their backs in the night.

~

Rachel pulled the boiling pot from the stove and set it between them to cool. Her question about their son still hung in the air between them.

"I want to come back home," he said.

"It's not your home anymore," she said and paused. She asked again, "What happened to Joaquin?"

"He didn't make it," Alcide said.

"Is that his blood?" she asked, pointing to the stains smeared across Alcide's coat.

In his memory, he saw every child she had birthed, and every bloody cloth buried under the oak tree behind their home.

"How did my son die?" She strained each word into existence, forcing it past the emotion in her throat.

"He was shot," Alcide said. "I was too late to save him. He tried to escape the camp with a some of the younger men," he continued. "Then the guards shot him." He had practiced the story over and over. After the prison camp was disbanded, he practiced those words along every step of his journey home. But sitting in front of the boy's mother, telling her the story, he felt as if he were watching Joaquin die all over again.

"I told you he was yours to protect," Rachel said.

His gut began to burn, and he thought he would be sick right here, on the table. "When you're in a bad spot, folks always say to remember the good things in your life. But they don't tell you those things start to slip away from you. Until one day, you wake up and wonder if there's any memory good enough to keep you tied to this earth."

Rachel stared into her coffee. The last bit of steam rose from the cup then disappeared. Finally, she said, "There's no place for you here, Alcide."

"You can't imagine what we did to stay alive," he said. "You can't imagine what I did to protect Joaquin."

"Don't say his name." she said.

Alcide gathered his coat and stood up from the table. He thought he would see a brokenness or sorrow in his Rachel's face. But there was something like relief washing over her face. He wondered if the relief was from having closure for their son.

He turned and said to her, "Try to remember us like we were before." Then he opened the back door and walked through it for the last time.

It had rained for three days before the night of Joaquin's death. The ground beneath their tents was sloppy and loose. Every step across the camp was a struggle for the emaciated men, and they found themselves sharing their beds with all manner of insects looking for a dry patch of ground in the deluge. But that night, the rain finally stopped, and the stars bloomed across the mountain sky. That night, Alcide and Joaquin lay quiet and still in their tent, listening to the wind carry the night sounds through the camp.

Sometime in the gray morning hours, Alcide heard men shouting and boots clomping through the mud. He opened his eyes to find that he was alone in the tent. He rushed outside to see the young men charging and killing, taking down every guard in their path. At the front of the pack, he saw his son, Joaquin, running a stolen bayonet through the belly of one of the guards. He cut another guard across the chest and began swinging his blade in every direction. The boy was unrecognizable now, an engine of hate covered in blood, and Alcide was afraid for him, not just for his safety, but for his soul.

He called out for his son, but his cry was cut short. A volley of gunfire erupted from behind him, and the prisoners began dropping one by one as the bullets pierced their ragged bodies. When the shooting stopped, Alcide was still screaming. He rushed to the scene, sifting amongst the union and confederate dead, each one huddled and indistinguishable from another. And there he found Joaquin.

He cradled his son's head close to his chest. Joaquin's body was pocked with holes, each one filling up with blood. He coughed, spewing blood onto Alcide's coat. He felt Joaquin's hand grasp his own, and his son tried to speak. Before he could, a group of guards rushed over and pulled Alcide from the mass of bodies. One of them pressed a rifle against Joaquin's head and pulled the trigger. The shot rang longer and louder than any before it. Alcide screamed for his son to get up, but Joaquin lay contented and still among the others, his eyes wide open and just as clear and green as the day they first opened.

~

The daylight was almost gone. As he walked towards the dead fields, Alcide rummaged through the barn behind the house. He emerged with two oak boards, nails, and a sturdy length of rope. He walked past the perished rows of beans and okra, his old crops gone to waste. Each step onto his old property felt like trespassing. The land that his family had cleared, nurtured, and cultivated was lost to him. He had become an exile, banished from paradise because of his sins. As he made his way onto his family's land, Rachel's words began to burrow themselves into his mind and spirit

There's no place for you here, Alcide.

At the edge of the fields, the ancient oak tree rose from the horizon line. Even at this distance and in the fading light he could see the grave markers under the shade of the tree. The first few sat straight and proud, carved from stone. In the tallest stone was etched the name of their first-born child, Emmaline. But down the line, the stones gave way to roughhewn crosses, sagging from time and humidity, with no names to bear.

Alcide found a large, sharp stone and used it to hammer the boards into a cross. With the sharp end of the stone, he etched his son's name, deep and bold, into the surface of the cross and drove it into the dirt.

There's no place for you here, Alcide

Alcide took off his coat and tore the confederate insignia from the shoulder and tossed it into the fields beyond the grave markers. He laid the coat on the ground in front of his son's new grave marker, the blood stain facing up toward the evening sky. He threw one end of the rope over a low branch in the oak tree and tied it into place. Alcide closed his eyes, and in his memory, he saw his family. There was Rachel, screaming in labor as Joaquin broke free from her body. Now, the boy was learning to push a plow and guide the mule in a straight line, making way for future crop yields. Now, he saw all their children, no longer buried but healthy and strong, gathered in a line in front of their home. At the head of the line was Joaquin. With a wave of his arm, he led them off into the sunset, his vibrant green eyes piercing through the evening darkness.

As he looped the rope around his neck, Alcide swore he could hear children playing in the distance, their laughter carried on the summer breeze.

Caretta, Caretta

When I was a kid, my parents and I spent every summer at Folly Beach. The three of us would make the three hour trip from the South Carolina upstate and spend a week on the beach. We wouldn't go sightseeing in nearby Charleston or visit historical areas. We just lazed in the sun for days. The only activity we ever took up was riding bikes under the oaks and palms lining the side streets. The sound of the waves roared over the dunes, and the gull calls mixed with all the other bird noises and marked the rise and fall of each day, and every night I walked the beach looking for fiddler crabs and turtle nests. Sometimes when I think about those vacations, I think about Mom and how she'd smile at me and act like Dad didn't exist at all. I think about how after my tenth birthday, she left us for good.

Every time we went to the beach, I brought an extra bag for seashells and other collectibles. By the end of each trip, I carried two full bags of seaside memorabilia. While the other kids ran through the surf and splashed in the tide pools, I walked up and down the shore, picking up shells, skeletons, and anything smooth or pearlescent. I waded into the water as well, just to see the flash of fish cross my path or the glint of a jellyfish pulsating through the sand and the water. I'd run back to my parents, both sitting underneath a blue and white umbrella, and show them what I'd found. Dad asked about each one while Mom rubbed lotion across her bronzing skin. She'd smile down at me and ask if I was having fun. Looking back now, it's all terribly depressing. Dad would pretend to be interested in my finds, while Mom really couldn't care any less. She already knew she was leaving at that point. She was waiting for the right time to do it. But now, even with the impending loneliness in that memory, I still remember being together.

Ten years after she left us, I'm back in Folly Beach. I'm not on vacation though. I live here. I'm not rich or a local merchant or anything glamorous. I'm a College of Charleston dropout who collects parking fares. I have an official polo shirt, an all-terrain golf cart, and the ability to write parking tickets on behalf of the city of Folly Beach. That's what I'm doing this morning. A green sedan is parked in front of a fire hydrant just a block from the beach. The hydrant is hidden behind a patch of bushes, but I know it's there and so does every other parking official. This city practically runs on parking fines. We ticket parked cars if one tire is even a quarter inch onto the pavement. The fine for parking in front of a fire hydrant is $250. I write a ticket for $125.

As I look to the saw grass marking the start of the beach, I see her. She's no older than six, maybe seven. The air is already hazy in the summer heat, even just across the road she's out of focus. The wind is carrying that salt smell over the man-made dunes, just enough of it to stick to your skin. I cross the road and when I squat down, she doesn't look up at me. Her bright green shorts are covered in sand, and her t-shirt is too big, probably a hand-me-down. She's piling sand on top of a children's book about sea turtles. The pages are made of kid-friendly cardboard, and the entire book is as thick as a large stack of quarters.

"Little girl," I say. She ignores me, so I repeat myself. The second time she looks up, puzzled as if the sand had come to life and started a conversation. She has eyes as big as a Bigeye Tuna, a *Thunnus Obesus.* Her blonde hair is scattered, and I see the large sea turtle on the cover of her book peeking out from underneath the sand.

"Where are your parents?" I ask.

"Knock, knock," she responds.

I can barely hear her over the gulls cawing to life around us. Even though I don't want to, I instinctively respond with "who's there?" I can't think of a better way to respond to a child telling a knock, knock joke, so I let it go and wipe the sweat from my neck.

"Canoe."

"Canoe who?"

"Canoe let me inside? It's cold out here." Without smiling or laughing, she goes back to burying her book.

I laugh at the joke, partly because I want to go back into the shade and partly because it's a mildly funny joke. "What's your name?" I ask. "Where are you from?" I look at her book and see that she's piling sand on top of a picture of a turtle egg. She doesn't respond to my questions, so I grab my radio and tell Herman at dispatch that I've got a lost child. Lost children are as common as sunburn at the beach. They wander off on their own, or some over-excited parent misplaces them. She seems like a wanderer. I give Herman a description of the girl, and when I look down she's tearing up blades of saw grass, sprinkling them over her bare feet.

"Do you like turtles?" I ask the girl.

She nods.

"Have you ever seen one?"

She shakes her head. "They bury their eggs."

"That's true," I say, relieved that she didn't tell another joke. "After it hatches, a baby sea turtle is only a few inches long. They're called hatchlings."

"How do you know that?" she asks with legitimate curiosity.

There's a long answer to that question, one that involves two years of studying marine biology, flunking out of college, an absentee mother, a mountain of student debt, and menial jobs. I decide to give her the short answer.

"Because I'm smart." I point to the picture of the egg that she's buried in the sand. "Are you trying to hatch that one?"

She looks at me incredulously. "It's not a real egg, silly."

Herman crackles through the radio, saying to bring her in, but to check boxes six through nine on the way, that he'd put her information onto the radio waves. It's not unusual for him to make me collect parking fares first. They're our first priority during the tourist season. I've got to check the parking boxes before the 10 am rush. If people can't jam their wadded up dollar bills into the slots, they won't pay. And then the city would go broke and it would be my fault, or that's how Herman would tell it. I've got to get things moving with this little girl. "What are your parents' names?" I ask.

She contemplates the question, brushes the sand off of the book, then tucks it under her tiny pink arm. "Knock, knock," she says.

~

I flunked out of college during my sophomore year. As my grades were falling, I started using ADHD medication to enhance my study time. The first time I used was the night before an Organic Chemistry midterm. My roommates said I'd taken too much, but I didn't care. I only cared about the chapter on entropy. It was only five pages long, but I memorized every word. What I didn't realize at the time was that the test wasn't on entropy. It was on alkenes, simple bonded structures. But I couldn't focus on anything but entropy. One paragraph described how everything in the universe is slowly falling apart. All of a sudden, I was afraid for my life because the universe and matter would eventually disband into nothingness. After the panic set in, I tore apart my room, looking for a box of old photos. I dug until I found the photo of Mom and Dad and me at the beach, the last photo I had of her. I studied every color and grain of sand and each one of my crooked little teeth. I memorized the wrinkles in Dad's shorts, the stripes and folds of Mom's tankini and oversized hat, and the shadows that all three of us made as we huddled underneath an umbrella. The sun glared behind us, but we were all smiling. And as I came down from the panic and the medication, I wept.

~

The girl and I have been riding up and down the coastline in my city issued golf cart. In an hour it will need to be charged, so I have to find her parents before then. I'm listening to the radio chatter for missing children from other parts of the beach. There've been several this morning. Two girls, but neither who matched her description. They were dark haired; she is blonde. They were nine or ten, but she looks closer to seven. They were wearing pink or purple swimsuits. She's wearing an oversized t-shirt and green cotton shorts. The other missing children weren't described as carrying a book on sea turtles either. She hasn't put hers down.

She's on her second read through of the book. I'm moving up Arctic Avenue (a truly ironic name for a road that borders the beach) and watching tourists come to seek the "Edge of America" as it's called on the maps. The beach rats are heading back to their houses or trailers, escaping the steady mob of tourists. A man crosses the street in front of us carrying two beach chairs on his back. He stops to call to his kids, and I stick the brake to the floor, jerking us to a stop. He waves. When he turns around I flip him the bird. He ducks underneath the shade of the palm trees that are sprouting amongst the oaks and dogwoods, then heads on to the pier steps. He waddles like a hermit crab. *Pargurus Bernhardus.* Most mornings I try and remember the classifications of various sea creatures. This morning, I'm on a roll.

I turn and again ask the girl what her name is again.

"Knock, knock," she says.

"Who's there?"

"Dwayne."

"Is that your name? That's a funny name for a girl," I say, trying to make a joke of it.

"Knock, knock."

I sigh. "Who's there?"

"Dwayne."

"Dwayne who?"

"Dwayne the bathtub. I'm drowning." She chuckles to herself then turns the page in her book.

Up ahead is one of my last three parking boxes. I pull to the shoulder, straddling the asphalt and the sand. "Come with me," I say and hand her the lockbox for the cash. To my surprise, she follows me. I unlock the box, and count the number of bills for each space. Everyone is paid-up except for space number five. There's a red Jeep parked in space five, but no money in the slot. The Jeep looks familiar, but I'm not sure why. There's a College of Charleston parking sticker on the front windshield and Connecticut plates. That's how I know it. He lived two houses down from me, a dark-haired Yankee with a passion for late-night ping-pong games and redheads. They seemed to be leaving that house almost every morning. I turn to the little girl, still holding the lockbox like a poor church orphan.

"Can you write?" I ask, miming with my hand. She nods.

As we hop back into the golf cart, I laugh thinking about the girl's elementary scrawl on an official city document. The ticket has my number on it, and it's on my route. There will be reprimands. But I don't care anymore.

"Do you like Italian Ice?" I ask.

She nods.

~

Sometime before she left me and Dad, Mom and I used to spend afternoons together in the garden. I don't remember how long we spent outside or what we were planting, I just remember the smell of dirt and the warmth of sunshine. Whenever I come across that smell, real dirt, black and moist, I think about her. When I think about her, I can hear her voice. She used to sing in the garden. Somewhere, in some magazine I think, she'd read that plants grow better when you sing to them. I'd listen to her soprano voice climb over the small rectangle of plants while she made holes in the dirt with a spade. Over time though, the songs changed.

The first one I remember was "Keep on the Sunny Side." She'd whistle it then sing it into the summer air. But as the days got shorter and colder, the songs changed too. I remember one that had a line about someone's face turning a whiter shade of pale. I remember it because the melody was the saddest I'd ever heard. She'd pull weeds from the dirt, grabbing the stalk at the base, and hum the tune between the lyrics, haphazardly flinging dirt on my hands and arms, burying them in the topsoil. One time I asked her to teach me the song so I could sing along with her.

She smiled and said, "Mommy likes to sing alone, sweetie."

Change has always bothered me. You can't see it or mark it in time, but it's irreversible, like smoke going up a chimney and out into the wider world. Mom started changing that year, the year I was ten. She changed without us, me and Dad. She went up the chimney alone and left us to sit and wait, to fend for ourselves. And now whenever I smell rich dark soil I think about that song and about Mom, the solo singer.

We're just a block from the Italian Ice stand now. The girl is scraping her feet back and forth across the floorboard of the golf cart through the fine layer of sand, making that scratching sound. The sand is everywhere here. You come to deal with sand being in your bed, your carpet, even the fridge. After a while, most people either move farther inland or they just deal with it. I don't notice it anymore.

I glance over at her to see a two page spread on the loggerhead turtle, *Caretta Caretta*. Her book doesn't say that, but I know the genus classification. I figure that she must be looking for turtles out here. That must be why she wandered from her parents. It's rare that any would nest this far north. The females come to shore to lay eggs and leave the young ones to fend for themselves. I don't tell the girl that. I don't tell her that *Caretta Caretta* is an endangered species, prized for its meat and eggs in places like Mexico. I don't tell her that she's at the wrong beach for turtles. Here on Folly Beach, there are no recorded turtle nests. Mostly they're all on Isle of Palms or Sullivan's Island. Even so, there are fewer and fewer nests every year. I don't tell her that they're becoming a rarity. I do tell her the Latin name for Loggerheads and that they're South Carolina's state reptile.

"*Caretta, Caretta*." She repeats the name carefully, as if trying to memorize each small movement of the tongue. She pauses for a moment. "Why do the mommas leave?" she asks.

"Nature tells them to."

"I don't think they would make good mothers anyway," she says in a matter of fact tone.

Without meaning to, I say. "My mother would've made a great sea turtle."

She doesn't acknowledge my comment. She's staring at a bright pink house. The paint is peeling off and the windows have a fine layer of film on them from the salt in the air.

"What's this one?" she asks, pointing to another picture.

"Leatherback turtle." She blinks at me, waiting for something else. "*Dermochelys coriacea*," I say. I explain the difference between the two turtles, the Leatherback and the Loggerhead, how they have different types of shells. Leatherback turtles have softer shells, like hard leather, whereas Loggerheads have a more traditional shell density. She is riveted, and for the first time I have her full attention. I should ask about her parents, but, for some reason, it doesn't seem like the right thing to ask. Plus, I've heard my fair share of knock, knock jokes.

She pauses, contemplating the turtles, I think. Then, she surprises me.

"My mom would make a good turtle too," she says.

For a moment, I'm not sure how to proceed.

"Why is that?" I ask.

"I don't get to see her in real life anymore." She stares at the picture of the turtle. In the picture, the hatchling is sliding into the surf, leaving a definite trench in the sand behind it. I think about putting my hand on her shoulder or telling her that it's going to be okay, but I can't because I don't know for sure. I don't know that she'll turn out okay or that she won't end up just like her mom or mine, our great vanishing sea turtle mothers.

I catch a whiff of soil on the wind, some enterprising homeowner who wants to grow the biggest hedges probably. But it takes me back. I think about Mom, and suddenly I hate her. I've tried my best over the years to not think about her, but I haven't been very consistent. The feeling fills me up, and I hate her for everything that's happened to me, things she has no idea about. I hate her for every terrible decision I've made and every equally terrible result. I hate her for leaving this little girl by herself on the beach, in the sun and the heat, to fend for herself with nothing but oversized clothes and a book of sea turtles. I hate her because through all my hate, I'm still content with everything that's happened to me.

The girl reaches the end of her book, then flips the pages back over to start again.

~

I make good on my promise of Italian Ice. I order cherry, and she requests a rainbow concoction of grape, strawberry, pineapple, blueberry, orange, and watermelon. The cart girl doesn't do a good job of the stripes, so her ice looks brown. I'm moving through mine quicker than I should. The sun is beating down on us now, and I'm sweating more than normal.

"How many Caretta Carrettas are there?" she asks, putting special emphasis on the "t" sound.

"They're endangered. There's less than there should be," I say.

"When the hatchlings are born, where is the daddy turtle?"

I'm impressed by her memory of the word "hatchling." I'm also not sure how to answer that question. Once the male turtle mounts the female, he's beaten up by the other males, sometimes killed. The answer to her question is probably that the daddy turtle is off healing up for his next lay. But I can't tell her that. I can't tell her that nature is cruel and stacked against creatures like her.

"He's off waiting for them. He wants the hatchlings to make it to the water, and then they swim off into the ocean together as a family."

She looks at me, and I know that she knows that I'm lying. But she has more grace than most people, so she says, "Knock, knock."

"Who's there?"

"I am."

For a moment, I think I may finally get this little girl's name, that she'll be open and honest with me, so I say, "I am who?"

"Did you forget who you are?" she says and then she laughs at her own joke the way that children do, and I laugh too. We're both laughing while the Italian ice girl scrolls through her phone. We laugh as the tourist families in their hats and sunscreen and rubber flip-flops stride by in the heat of the day. We laugh, and I forget that this girl has a family somewhere out there looking for her, maybe even worried about her.

We walk across the road to the beach. She wants to see where the turtles cross the sand on their way to the water. We're sitting near one of the concrete barricades that lend stability to the sand and serves as a home for graffiti messages. Ours reads "Class of '08."

The girl is smiling, watching the waves roll and break on the bronze sand. Other supervised children are wading in the tide pools just ten feet from the surf, but she doesn't seem jealous, only content to watch the water from a distance.

"Turtles lay their eggs this far back?" she asks.

"Sometimes," I say, although it's true. We're nearly twenty yards from the water. Seagulls are landing and taking off, searching for stray picnic pieces and brave hermit crabs. I think about thirty or so hatchlings, all boiling out of the sand at once. They'll surface in the dead of night, start from the beach grass, and make their way toward the moonlight, slowly flapping their way to the water. I suppose the journey makes them stronger, but nature has never been that kind or poetic.

As I'm daydreaming, the girl sets her ice cone down and walks toward the water. She's dragging her feet, leaving small trenches in the sand and broken shells. The sun is falling behind us and casts her shadow long and skinny, a needle of a girl shuffling to the waves. The radio on my belt crackles and Herman says he thinks he's found the girl's father, that he described her down to the shorts and turtle book. I unclip the radio and set it in the sand.

I stand so I can see the girl across the twenty or so yards of shoreline. The tourists slowly pack it all in and head for their cars. Her green shorts are visible, and she's dangling that turtle book by one hand. My radio is still squawking, Harold looking for a response. I tell him we're on our way back, then set it in the sand. Soon I'll grab her by the hand and lead her back to her dad. But for now, I'm watching those small trenches she made, as the girl makes her way into the rising surf.

Everything That We've Buried

The old timers around Moncks Corner always liked to tell me about what's buried underneath Lake Moultrie. A whole other town that was flooded when the Santee and Cooper Rivers were dammed up to make cheap electricity. And a fair share of those old timers have little pieces of that place hanging up in their garages or their living rooms. Little pieces that, every now and then, would float to the surface for some lucky boater to scoop up and bring home. Things like a fence post or a roof shingle. Some folks held that everything down there would come up eventually. Said it was some sort of natural law. Of course, sometimes things that came up weren't worth putting on a wall.

It was the gunshots that drew all the attention. I got a call on the radio about multiple shotgun blasts somewhere near Lyons Beach on the east side of the lake. Said it'd been going on for about a half hour or so. I parked my sheriff's cruiser next to two paramedics waiting in their ambulance, lights twirling and engine idling in an empty lot, just out of view of the beach. I knocked on the driver's window. The driver, a boy I only knew by reputation, opened the door and let an avalanche of cool air roll into my sopping wet face.

"Bout time," he said.

"Y'all waiting for me?" I asked. A gun shot echoed through the empty morning air.

"Owen called in about his old man. We got here and heard the shots. Been going off ever couple minutes."

I recognized the other paramedic right away. "How you doing there, Sam?" I asked.

"Alright, Howard," he said without making eye contact. "How's your daddy?"

"Good," I said, turning to the beach. "Thanks for asking." It's one of those things that you have to do in a small community, make small talk with folks even if you don't particularly care to talk to them. Or even if you've got some kind of nasty history like me and Sam Hartigan had. But, it's water under the bridge, as they say.

Another shot rang out in the summer air. The other paramedic motioned like a maître d showing me to the best table in the house, so I figured I might as well see what all the hoopla was about.

Owen Mathis was about two years my younger, same age as my late brother Robbie, but his face was marked by his work. Spending most of his life hunched over a dying crop of peas and soybeans had aged him by at least ten years. And not just his looks. He carried that quiet stoic air about him that old men have. The earned currency of silence, as our daddy used to say before he quit saying anything at all.

It really was quite a sight to see, Owen standing over his daddy's body, still soaking wet, staring up into the sun while a flock of bald-headed buzzards circled overhead. Every few seconds, he'd rear the gun up and blast another load of buckshot into the sky and the steady moving circle would scatter, then come back together in perfect unison. When I got within earshot, he filled me in.

"Found him here, washed up. Damn birds was pecking through his clothes," Owen said.

"Paramedics said you called it in," I said, watching the mass of black feathers hovering above us.

Owen broke open the barrel and loaded in another two shells. "Daddy said he was going boating last night. I woke up and he wasn't back. Found him floating here by the dock."

"I reckon he slipped in and drowned," I said trying to be helpful. "Was he drinking?"

Owen aimed the barrel into the sky. "Only when he wasn't sleeping." He squeezed the trigger of the shotgun, sending a fresh spray of lead into the circle of hungry birds. The circle broke, then came back together.

I spoke as loud as I could so as to hear myself over the ringing in my ears. "Paramedics gotta come in and do their thing. Otis is better off with them than lying in the sun like this."

"Sam out there?" he asked reloading.

"Yeah," I said.

Owen gave me a side eyed look then took aim again into the sky. "You're a better man than me."

"I got no quarrel with him," I said, tracking the birds over our heads. It reminded me of something I'd read in school, but I couldn't place it right away.

"If a man killed my brother," he said. "I'd of put him in the ground long time ago." He fired another round of buck shot. Feathers broke. Feathers came back together. "Just keep coming back, don't they?"

"Turning in the widening gyre," I said.

Owen threw another side eyed look at me.

"Something I read once." I stepped in a little closer. "Why don't you just set the gun down and go cool down in the cruiser," I said. "I'll watch your daddy. Make sure the birds stay up there."

He looked at me for a good minute, then handed over the shotgun. I watched him walk back towards the ambulance in the morning heat. I wondered what folks would make of this scene: me standing there holding a shotgun with a drowned body at my feet and a circle of buzzards over my head. I thought about what else might be buried in that lake, what other unexpected things might be waiting to make their way up to the surface.

~

That night I made dinner for me and Daddy. I sent his nurse home early and set the table. It reminded me of being a kid again, everything in its proper place. But not everyone, not since Robbie left us.

Daddy sat in his wheelchair at the other end of a six-seater table made from a sturdy white oak tree that was probably older than the United States of America. Daddy spent the month before Robbie was born building that table for the whole family to eat at. He was so excited that he let me help him some. But two days after Robbie was born, Daddy buried his wife and took home two sons to raise on his own.

"Otis Mathis died this morning," I said, watching Daddy pull the fork to his mouth. The shaking in his hands scattered a few grains of rice over the plate.

"Got drunk and drowned in the lake. He was about your age." Daddy kept focus on the rice shaking through the gaps in his fork. His stroke side, as I called it, hung loose like a shirt stretched too hard at the collar.

"Owen was shooting that over-under shotgun his granddaddy left him," I continued, "trying to scare away the buzzards." Daddy's face was stone, that same stoic look I saw in Owen that morning. So I tried something else.

"Sam Hartigan was there," I said.

Daddy perked up, his eyes lit up and flickered like the old gas lamps down in Charleston. "Nance," he said. "Nance. Nance. Nance."

"I didn't say much to him," I said, ignoring our mother's name. It was the only thing he could say anymore. "He looked surprised to see me," I said.

Daddy kept on. "Nance. Nance," getting louder and louder with each mention of our dead mother's name. Only he had ever called her Nance. She was Nancy to everyone else. I don't remember much about her being as I was only about two when she passed after giving birth to Robbie. She's beautiful in all the pictures. Doctors said that Daddy might've been fixated on her when the stroke hit and got her name lodged in his brain like a bad dream.

"I always wondered," I said between mouthfuls of rice and stewed tomatoes, "what I would do if I saw him, Sam I mean."

"Nance. Nance."

"I ain't one to hold a grudge though. The past is in the past. Nothing we can do to change it."

"Nance."

I let Momma's name hang in the air between us for a minute. I replayed that short exchange me and Sam had. The niceties and social protocols we obeyed.

I cleaned up the kitchen and helped Daddy bathe and got him settled into bed. In the empty living room, I sat in his old leather recliner and put one of his old 45s on to play. A voice scratched to life singing about Sunday mornings and disappearing yesterdays. And I let the lonely melody carry me down.

~

It was a Thursday night when Robbie died. His truck hit a seven-point deer bounding across the road on a blind turn in the darkest part of the night on the darkest corner of the whole damned county. Robbie tried to swerve out of the way of the deer when he saw it, but the animal was too big. The truck clipped the deer then swerved into a ditch and rolled three times over in front of Miss Mable Clarke's house. The old widow only heard the tires screeching and the glass breaking. She told the police she thought someone was breaking into her house and came outside with her late husband's hunting rifle, ready to kill someone.

Robbie was working the late shift at the Santee Cooper power plant. He'd been higher than a goddamn kite when he came to that turn. My younger brother had a penchant, like most folks in this area, for mixing pills and whiskey. He used to say he was trying to get the most out of his life. The irony there hasn't been lost on me.

But the accident didn't kill him. I was on scene not two minutes after I heard the call come over the radio. I saw my mangled brother with my own eyes and he spoke to me. He kept telling me not to look in the glovebox, smiling the whole time. I assumed it was a stash of whatever he was high on at the time. On scene they said he had a few deep cuts, broke his shoulder and a few ribs, some internal bruising and minor bleeding along with a nasty concussion. But he was alive when they loaded him in the ambulance. He was alive when he told me he didn't want me riding in the ambulance, that he was a big boy now, and when he flashed that crooked smile. But by the time he got to the hospital, he was bleeding out and heading into heart failure.

The coroner labeled Robbie's death as "due to injuries." The report said he'd bled out into his chest cavity on the way to the hospital. They said by the time they got him on the table the blood had gotten into his lungs and within a few minutes he had drowned in the stuff.

Then, a few weeks later, the paramedic who had loaded Robbie into the ambulance, a young fellow named Sam Hartigan, got high and cried to a local working girl about how he killed some poor boy in the back of his ambulance. He was at the illegal bar on Lyons Beach near the lake. He was apparently sobbing, saying he gave him the wrong injection and caused him to bleed out. Talked about the boy coughing up blood, the gurgling sound he kept making. By the next morning, the news had traveled around the county till everyone and their momma knew that Sam Hartigan had killed my brother because he'd been too panicked to realize he'd given blood thinner to a man with internal injuries.

But gossip ain't a burden of proof. And even though he'd probably killed my brother, he was protected by the coroner's report. Got to keep his job and everything. But it was never the same for Sam. The whole town had heard the story and knew he was the man who had probably killed Robbie McCormack. Folks started whispering about him wherever he went and most everyone didn't want nothing to do with him anymore. He was alone. And for a while, I think, that was enough for me.

~

I shot awake, still sitting in Daddy's chair and still fully dressed. The record had ended, throwing that empty scratching noise all around me. I had dreamed the whole damn thing over again. The wreck, Robbie's death, Sam's confession, all of it. That day at the lake was first time I'd seen Sam since the night Robbie died the year before. We'd been lucky enough to avoid each other. And no matter how many folks asked, I always said the same thing. Mistakes were made. Revenge wouldn't change anything. But that right then, I sat in that chair waiting for the night to pass me by, wondering if Sam was as distraught as I was right that moment, playing everything over again like I had. I got up and reset the record back to the start again.

~

Two days later I went to visit Owen Mathis at his daddy's wake. I came straight from my patrol and wandered through their house like a khaki island lost in a sea of black dresses and crocodile tears. I shook hands with folks I knew and nodded to those I didn't, all the while thinking about the scene just a few days earlier. Otis laying face down in the sand with a flock of flesh-eating birds hovering about, waiting to pick him apart. Not exactly a conversation starter.

I spotted Owen on the back porch, smoking and staring off into the distance with his shirt sleeves rolled as high as they'd go. I stepped outside to shake his hand.

"I'm sorry about your daddy," I said over the cicadas humming all around us. A thick cloud was moving over the horizon, bringing a batch of heat lightening with it and the welcome threat of summer rain.

"Me too," he said.

"You got everything you need?" I asked, not knowing why.

He took a long pull off the cigarette and blew it out his nose. After a few moments he went on. "Who's to blame for all this?"

"It was just an accident," I said, a little lost.

"That's why you're so lucky."

"Nobody's lucky in death, Owen."

He perked up, and for the first time I could smell the whiskey seeping from his skin.

"Don't you don't ever hear a song and think, I bet Robbie would love this song and then have to remind yourself that he's gone? It doesn't make you angry that there's someone out there who's responsible for that feeling?"

A dull rumble of thunder came through the clouds. It was miles off, but I wanted it to come as quickly as possible now.

"I suppose I get that way, sure" I confessed.

"It's all just stirring up underneath. The blame and the anger. Waiting to come out." He took another drag from the cigarette. "And when it comes up, I got nowhere to put it all. That's why you're lucky."

"Revenge doesn't change anything." I knew the line by heart now, and I repeated it like an actor on a very familiar stage.

"Bullshit," Owen said watching the same storm building upwards over the horizon. "You push it down, act like it's not there. But it'll come up eventually. Even you with your shiny badge." Another roll of thunder washed over the porch where we stood. "It's a law of nature," he said. And then everything else was still and quiet.

"I suppose you're right," I said, trying to end the conversation as peacefully as I could.

"Take me back inside," Owen said. And I led him back into his father's house.

~

Growing up in the country, you get used to wide open spaces. My favorite places around Moncks Corner are the ones I end up in by myself, not another soul for miles in any direction. You get used to having that luxury after a while. So when you find yourself at a crowded wake, twenty people feels like a hundred, and you get a bit antsy. Not to mention the emotion of it all.

I led Owen to a couch then shoved my way out the door and collapsed into my cruiser, giving myself just a minute to breathe in the aloneness. After a minute, I fired up the car and headed back toward town.

I was supposed to go to the station, drop off the cruiser, change out of my uniform and head home. But I kept driving. All the way down Black Tom Road where Owen lived and back out to Highway 52. I followed the highway past the Sheriff's station to the lake and cruised along the roads bordering the beach. I thought about those old timers, the ones who talk about the homes and fields buried under thirty feet of man-made lake. I thought about the pieces of that world floating to the surface and making their way into our world. Things that were decomposed or thought to be long dead that eventually broke free, that wouldn't stay buried no matter how hard the rest of world tried to make them stay that way.

And as I turned a corner, I came to the illegal bar right off Lyons Beach. You'd never know it was there if you didn't already know about it. The building is unmarked and cinderblock like everything else around, with two windows, surrounded by makeshift homes on every side. The place was only big enough to fit ten, maybe fifteen people at a time. But there was nowhere else to get local shine or pick up a few tabs of this or that. The Sheriff's department had been out here a good bit, but it never seemed to make much difference. The place would shut down for a while then come back to life when you weren't looking.

Without knowing why, I pulled into a lot across the street, far enough away so as not to look suspicious, but anyone with half an eyeball could see the Berkeley County Sheriff's logo blazed across the side of my car. I parked, and I waited, smelling the lake wind rolling through the cab, trying to convince myself that I was there to enjoy the rest of my evening, to be alone finally.

From across the street I saw a man making his way toward the bar. I knew who he was, even without looking at the EMS logo on his shoulder patch. He walked across the lot and towards the bar with a purpose in his step and, no doubt, a plan for how the rest of his evening would go.

So I climbed out of my car, the sunlight draining away into the night, and called him by name.

~

When I got home that evening, Daddy was still up, sitting in his cracked leather chair. In the corner his old record player was spinning a tune I didn't recognize, some lonely guitar and deep voice singing about loss and self-medication. I told the home nurse she could take off.

"Working late?" she asked as she packed up her things.

"Always."

When she left I sat on the yellow tweed sofa opposite Daddy, watched his eyes stare a hole into the base of the record player. I tucked my hands out of view for the moment.

"I did something tonight," I finally said.

He didn't respond. So I kept on.

"I only wanted to talk it out with him, you know?"

Daddy's eyes slid my direction.

"It's been near about a year. It's supposed to be water under the bridge. But when I saw him up close, staring at me." I took a breath, feeling all sorts of new emotions coming up out of my chest. "I asked him what he gave Robbie that night. And when he said he didn't know, I lost it. Everything just came pouring up out of me. When I caught him the first time in the nose and felt it crack, I wanted more. And he never fought back. He just took it. Kept saying 'I'm sorry' over and over again. And I kept on at him. Until everything was just wet."

Daddy's jaw started fidgeting, mouth opening and closing but nothing coming out. So I kept on.

"I didn't want any of this to happen. Revenge doesn't change anything," I said. The words came off my tongue, but there was no heart in them anymore, just a set of sounds and syllables with no real meaning. Because now, everything had changed.

The record came to an end, filling the room with that scratching sound.

"Everything's out in the open now."

Daddy threw a bit of spittle as he let out his customary, "Nance." I wiped his chin, stretching out the gashes and bruises on my hand. There was a pain deep below the skin that told me I'd broken a small and probably irreplaceable part of myself. The record kept turning, and Daddy kept trying to find his words, two empty sounds, nothing but noise.

Right then, I felt pity for my old daddy, for what the stroke had taken from him. I wondered what it was like to have so many ideas and words down inside you and have everything come up exactly the same. When you set out to say something meaningful, but despite all that intention there was something else waiting to spring out past your lips. And in that moment, all I could think of was the trickling flow of Sam's blood running down my hand and the steady circle of black feathers hovering above my head.

Zombie Jesus

Growing up in a fundamentalist Christian church, we were taught that Halloween was the Devil's high holiday. And, like all good fundamentalist Christians, my brother and I never went trick-or-treating. Every fall, we listened to the other kids in school debating costume choices, sharing the best routes, and planning their own candy-binge parties. Outwardly, we accepted our role as conscientious Christian objectors, and we even passively condemned those heretics and pagans. But at night, in the silence of my own thoughts, I wondered why God didn't want me to have any fun.

So in the sixth grade, I decided that I wouldn't let God keep me from having fun anymore. I told my parents that I wanted to go trick-or-treating and that I wanted to dress up as a Power Ranger. My father sat me down on our sofa and, with much patience and gentleness, began to summarize one of our pastor's sermons, explaining how the Devil and his minions twist the sinners' minds, causing them to put razor blades into apples or lace candy bars with crack-cocaine, and that when we wear costumes, we open ourselves to demonic attack and possession.

I asked my father how dressing as a Power Ranger could endanger my eternal soul.

He smiled and said, "Son, darkness has no fellowship with the light, and what is done in darkness, will be brought to light on the day of judgement."

As those words settled on me, I sat, too afraid to move. In that moment, God seemed like some wild predator, waiting for me to flinch so he could run me down and rip me apart for the glory of his kingdom. Needless to say, I did not go trick-or-treating.

That was the year my father felt the Holy Spirit calling our family to join the war against the forces of Satan. At the dinner table one night, he said, "This Halloween, we're going to tell the Devil that he is not welcome in this house." For the next two days, my father drove around the neighborhood, picking up any piece of scrap wood he could find then hauling it home. Every evening, after he locked himself in the garage, he asked us not to disturb him. Then the house would echo with the sounds of cutting and hammering, and the occasional profanity, followed by a quick, mumbled prayer of forgiveness.

On Halloween night, right at sunset, our father emerged from the garage, caked in dust and sweat, like how I imagined Jesus emerged from the tomb.

And with a sigh and a smile, my father said, "It is finished."

He rushed the three of us outside to the front yard and gestured proudly toward his creation: a seven-foot-tall crucifix, cobbled together out of scrap wood and spare nails, and splattered with fake blood. Upon that cross, my father had hung a life-sized zombie, a cheap plastic Halloween decoration, its arms stretched and nailed to the cross, its head topped with a woman's wig, completed with a crown of thorns. Our mother gasped, trying to catch what was left of her breath. From the foot of my father's cross, I gazed up at Zombie Jesus, and he looked back at me through gruesome, plastic eyes.

"What have you done?" asked our mother.

My father turned to her, and with the compassion of our savior, he said, "Now everyone in this neighborhood will know that we celebrate Jesus, not Halloween." With that, he flipped on a spotlight, illuminating his handiwork for the whole neighborhood to see. Then he led us back inside.

As Halloween night settled onto the neighborhood, unsuspecting trick-or-treaters walked past our house, some gawking and laughing at the Son of God re-crucified on our front lawn, others shielding their children's eyes and rushing them away to the next house. Inside, we huddled together on the couch, my father leading a prayer against the forces of Satan outside our door. My brother and I could only stare out the front window, as the light from Zombie Jesus bathed us in all its glory.

Chucklehead

Howard pulled the sheriff's cruiser to the side of the road closest to Rosseau's catfish farm. He was traveling south on highway 52 heading out of Moncks Corner. When he climbed out of the car, he took just a moment to look out over the gathering of small reservoirs. He supposed each one contained at least seven hundred to one thousand catfish, all swimming over top and underneath of each other, each one carving their own path through the murky water to be overlapped by his neighbor and the path erased. His brother Robbie called them chuckleheads, though he didn't know why. The more Howard thought about it, he'd never heard anyone else refer to a catfish as a chucklehead, only his brother. He wondered where it came from.

Howard scanned over the empty space of the reservoirs and the bottom feeders therein. He imagined them eating scraps of meat and other fish, living or dead, whatever happens to fall in their path. They consume without discretion, or at least, that was what he was once told. Apparently, catfish will eat anything that happens to sit still long enough. He had eaten fried catfish just last week, and he now wondered what sort of dead things that fish had eaten before being consumed itself. He laughed aloud, with no one else to hear.

"Chucklehead," he said. The word tasted like popcorn in his mouth. He said it again, then took a piss into the dirt.

Howard stood just over six feet tall. His grandmother said he was built like a bull on hind legs. His shoulders threatened the seams of nearly every shirt he owned, but his waist tapered down to a lean thirty inches. When he'd joined the Berkeley County Sheriff's office, they'd had to special order shoes for him. No one else in the department had ever worn a size thirteen. The first jokes made about Howard were whether or not he would fit in the cruiser. They said he looked like a circus clown when he climbed out of the car, legs like a spider and shoulders like a cypress trunk.

As he stood on the side of highway 52, urinating into a patch of grass, Howard looked out over the catfish farms in the distance. At least twenty bodies of water, some as large as a pond and others as small as a ditch, stretched across the flat ground.

He was still mulling over the word chucklehead, trying to figure where his brother first heard it, where it had come from. Howard finished his business and got back into his car. There was no air conditioning in the car, and the metal frame conducted so much heat that no matter where he went, Howard was always sweating. His pants stuck to the seat, and his shirt stuck to his back. His hat was already stained around the brim, a noticeable shade of dark discoloration around the circumference like a crown of the hard deeds he'd completed in his life.

Howard cranked the car, and the radio squawked to life. Someone was calling his number over the police frequency. The dispatcher, probably Rita, said that she had been trying to reach him for some time. He had been specifically requested by a clerk at Kryzinski's Hardware down on White Street. She said his brother Robbie had gotten into a scuffle with two of the King boys from Summerville. "You sure it was Robbie?" he asked the dispatcher, and she described his brother, white fellow, five eleven, black hair, missing one finger on his left hand and three of his bottom teeth.

"The teeth must be a new development," Howard said back.

He ignited the roof lights and pushed the engine has hard as he could down the highway. He thought about Robbie's teeth being newly removed, most likely because of this scuffle with the King brothers. Howard tried not to grit his own teeth, but he found himself grinding his molars so hard his jaw muscles flared and twitched through the skin.

"Goddamn chucklehead," he said.

When Howard pulled into Kryzinski's Hardware store, someone had wedged a shovel against the inside door handle and flipped the sign so it read "Sorry, We're Closed." He knocked on the glass, and a stout Hispanic woman half walked and half waddled up an aisle lined with PVC pipes and fittings. She removed the shovel from the door and let Howard inside. He saw that her hands were smeared with blood and her left fist looked as though it were clenched around something too precious to lose.

"Gracias, Nerida," he said in his country-fried Spanish. The woman did not respond, but simply glared at him.

Nerida, the shop owner, then shouted, in a deft mixture of English and Spanish, that if she ever saw any of them in here again, she'd call the real police, that this was the last time she would give Howard the courtesy of picking up his brother, that next time, she'd laugh as he rotted forever in a jail. Half of what Nerida said flew by him like an oncoming car. He only caught about every other word, until she threatened to "break Robbie's ass with a shovel." The department had trained them well on threats and cussing in Spanish but not much else. She waved the shovel about, still shooting Spanish from the hip like an old desperado. Nerida and her husband had moved to Moncks Corner after her husband lost his job as an Agave farmer in middle Mexico. They opened the hardware store and named it Kryzinski's. At the time, it was the most American sounding name they could think of.

Howard nodded and took a moment to process what she'd said. Howard only spoke what he called "emergency Spanish." For him, listening to it was like sifting through a bale of hay, tedious.

"*¿Donde estan?*" Howard asked. He never could get the Spanish accent down.

She led him to the back of the store, down the gardening aisle. The floor was littered with plastic parts and broken odds and ends, as though some wild animal had decided to nest in the aisle. The tile floor was smeared with blood, and it looked as though it had been cracked in places. Resting among a shallow puddle of water and blood was a door knocker, the letter 'S' stamped into the brass. The metal bore a bloody tint and the handle was bent slightly inward, in the shape of a man's grip.

In the back of the hardware store, three men were sitting on the floor, each one with his hands zip tied behind his back and his head bowed to the ground. For a moment Howard imagined they were all overgrown children, ashamed of what they had done. But he knew they weren't sorry, especially his brother, tucked away from the other two in a secluded corner of the back room like the cut-up who couldn't get along with the rest of the class. The King brothers were a collective disfigurement, two faces of the same mold with different spots of swelling and yellowing and bleeding. Howard didn't believe that the brothers, Carl and Huck, could even see him out of their swollen eyes, now raised to the shape of a pitcher's mound.

Howard asked Nerida how she managed to stop three grown men by herself. She replied that she just waited until all the beating stopped.

Huck King, the younger of the brothers, groaned and turned in a direction near Howard's voice. He tried to mumble out words, but instead drooled blood down his t-shirt. Carl, the older brother, tried to translate for his sibling, but his lips were swollen beyond use. He coughed, then let his head fall back down, the dribble of blood staining his skin.

Howard stepped over the Kings and crouched in front of his own brother, his head slack against the concrete wall behind him. Robbie's cheek was opened up like a ravine, and a creek of blood had begun to flow down to the corner of his mouth. Both of his lips had inflated to twice their normal size. He wiggled the nub on his right hand where his middle finger used to be. He'd lost it while playing with firecrackers as a child. He'd lit the fuse and held on for the sake of proving to Howard that he could outlast him. He held on for a few seconds too long. It exploded in his hand and blasted his middle finger off at the second knuckle. He and Howard had found the missing finger two days later in a ditch, undisturbed, almost thirty yards away.

"Wake up, chucklehead," Howard said to his brother, still slouched against the store wall. He wasn't sure why he called him chucklehead. It just came out. He patted his brother on the shoulder.

Robbie raised his head slightly. His forehead was smeared with blood and a chunk of hair was missing from his right side, just above his ear. His eyes were swollen shut. Howard could see the yellowing and bruising that spread across his face. Robbie moved his lips apart, then curled them into a pseudo-smile, in a way that reminded Howard of how alligators smile when they open their jaws. He jutted his own jaw forward and choked out, "Tell her I want them back."

Howard looked over at Nerida, her left hand still clenched tight. He walked over to her and held out his palm. "Él *quiere esos*," he said to her and pointed at her fist, sealed tight. She growled like a tomcat, then dropped three adult teeth into Howard's open hand. The roots were chipped and bloodied. They looked to Howard like seeds that would perhaps grow him a new brother, one with more sense and self-control.

He promised Nerida that Robbie wouldn't so much as walk by Kryzinski's anymore. Likewise, she promised that if she saw Robbie again, she would call the real police.

"We ain't got no *federales* on this side of the border, Nerida," Howard said.

"Then I'll beat him like he do to them," she replied, pointing at the King brothers. Howard had rarely ever heard her speak English. He took that as a sign that she was done with this foolishness.

Howard instructed her to cut the Kings loose as soon as he and Robbie were gone. Robbie tried to hobble himself to the car but fell into the gravel when he stepped off the curb. Howard picked his brother up and brushed the tiny rocks out of his facial wounds, then helped him the rest of the way. He drove slower than he had coming in. There didn't seem to be a rush anymore. Robbie sat slouched in the backseat, still clutching his three bottom teeth in his hand.

"Don't stain the upholstery," Howard said.

Robbie grunted.

"You been pestering the Kings again?" Howard asked.

Robbie smiled and coughed. "Me and Gary Driggers let a bunch of chickens loose in their porch. Whole place was covered in chickenshit by morning." Robbie breathed deep, then exhaled, a fine mist of spit and blood coating the seat in front of him.

"That's a new one," Howard said. Robbie and his friends had developed a long history of pestering the King brothers. Even in high school, the King brothers had feuded with Robbie and any number of his friends. When Carl and Huck King, no doubt empowered by their daddy's money and status, flexed their social posture against others, Robbie saw it as his duty to set the world straight. And like any immature, school-aged rivalry, things began to escalate beyond the school walls. Neither the King brothers nor Robbie had been in high school for nearly a half a decade. But bad blood, as Howard well knew, dies hard in young men.

"All this over some chickenshit?" Howard asked. "What happened in the store?" he added.

Robbie smirked back at him. He bounced his teeth in his hand like they were marbles and chuckled again. Finally, he said, "They hit like pussies." Then he added, "Don't take me to the clinic. I got plenty of pills at home."

"You can't tell me things like that. I'm still the law."

Robbie laughed then slouched back. "Blood before the badge, brother."

"They're probably not gonna press charges," Howard said.

"I know," Robbie said.

"You took things too far this time. Chickenshit and school-boy nonsense is one thing. This is a goddamn felony."

"Maybe I didn't take it far enough," Robbie said.

Howard tried to let his brother's words pass over him, but the lawman in him wouldn't let him just ignore a comment like that, no matter how much he wanted to protect Robbie.

"You proud of yourself?"

"'The LORD opposes the proud' brother," Robbie said.

Howard ignored the scripture reference, refusing to play his brother's games anymore.

"I'm serious," he said.

"Dad would be proud." Robbie kicked his foot against the passenger head rest and laid himself down across the backseat.

He looked like their father now, bloody and eerily relaxed. Howard could see their father's long legs and bony shoulders in his brother's frame. He could hear his aggression and insecurities in every syllable that spilled out of Robbie's mouth.

"Dad's a terrible role-model." Howard said and jerked the steering wheel. The cruiser skidded down an unmarked dirt road, a cloud of red dust trailing behind them.

"At least he's still breathing," Robbie said.

Howard pulled a cigarette from the pack in the passenger seat and lit the tip, desperately trying to busy his hands. As kids, he and Robbie had scrapped like young boys often do. He remembered the feel of his brother's nose crunching under the weight of his fist. The memory steadied his hands.

"No one ever blamed you for her," Howard said.

"Dad does."

Howard shifted in his seat, suddenly aware of the stifling heat radiating in the car. His own memories of their mother bubbled to the surface of his mind, the kind and loving woman who had shown him what mercy and grace looked like. The same woman that his brother Robbie had killed when he split her open at birth.

"I don't blame you," he said after a long silence.

"Maybe you should," Robbie said. "Maybe it's all my fault."

Howard let out a breath that sounded more like a growl. "You know what you are?" he said.

"What's that, Officer Fife?"

"A bottom feeder," Howard said. "A scavenger who just feeds on whatever others leave behind." He took a long drag from the cigarette and exhaled towards his brother's face.

Robbie waved away the second-hand smoke. "And I suppose you're the big fish? Big Howie bringing the peace. Keeping the nasty criminals of Berkeley County at bay."

"When was the last time you visited Dad?" Howard asked, knowing the wound it would cause in his brother. As close as they had been growing up, since their dad had started descending into dementia, Robbie had been absent from his house, leaving Howard to care for their father and to explain to him, almost every night, that his wife, their mother Nance, had died giving birth to Robbie.

"I've been busy," Robbie said, staring out the window and watching the empty landscape give way to dense pine forests.

"You're a fucking tragedy," Howard said.

He pulled the cruiser to a stop, just under the sign for Rousseau's Catfish Farm. He peeled his shirt, still slick with sweat, from his torso and rolled his massive frame out of the cruiser, grabbing his hat out of habit more than necessity. With one drag, he finished the cigarette between his teeth and threw the butt into the nearest catfish holding pond. He expected the fish to break the surface, looking for an easy meal. But they continued on their paths, circling the bottom of the pond, stirring up wakes of mud and shit with every twist of their tails.

He hadn't expected to come back here, but something about it felt right. Like most older siblings, Howard assumed responsibility for his younger brother's behavior. In the absence of their mother, maybe he should've been more supportive and caring. Maybe he should've hit him harder when they fought. Whatever his shortcomings were, Howard couldn't pick just one. His brother was a swirl of failures, some big and some small, but all of them now rising up to meet Howard everywhere he went.

"I should've left you in that store," he said.

Robbie now stood next to him, both of them staring at the catfish circling aimlessly in the holding pond. "Maybe you're right," he said. "Maybe I am just a bottom feeder. Destined to eat everyone else's leftovers and shit."

"Is that what you want?"

"Maybe it's what I deserve."

"You know," Howard said, still watching his cigarette butt floating to the bottom of the pond. "At the rate you're going, you'll be dead and buried before daddy. You can't be making enemies and picking fights forever."

Robbie smiled and wrapped his arm around his brother's broad shoulders. "Thou hast smitten my enemies upon the cheekbone," he said, smacking his fist into Howard's shoulder. "Thou hast broken the teeth of the ungodly." He jingled the loose teeth in his palm like old men jingle change. Howard would never admit it, but the sound of his brother's teeth rattling in his palm was a nice fit to the Bible verse. It always struck him as odd that someone as wild and unstable as his brother knew so much scripture.

Howard looked towards the setting sun, just beyond the trees that shielded the catfish farm from the road. "What exactly is a chucklehead?" he asked his brother.

Robbie looked at his brother as if he were asking the color of the sky. Robbie laughed and replied, "It's a catfish."

"I know that, but where did that word come from?" Howard fanned himself with his hat. "I've never heard anyone else call 'em that but you."

Robbie thought for a moment. Then a look came over him, as if he'd never considered the meaning and origin of the thing. The look of confusion and self-contemplation quickly vanished into a mostly-toothless grin. "Must've been one of those boys from up north. Just always stuck with me."

Howard considered what he was about to say. He felt the weight of the words in his mind and fought against himself for a few moments. Finally, he said to his brother, "I can't be there for you next time."

"If we're lucky," Robbie said with a cracked smile, "Next time'll be the last time."

Robbie slapped his brother on the back and started back towards the police cruiser.

"I'm serious," Howard called after him. "I can't save you anymore."

Robbie turned and extended the nub of his middle finger, then climbed into the back of the police cruiser in one smooth and practiced motion.

Howard watched the cigarette butt twirl and sway to the bottom of the pond. A passing catfish circled around it, then opened its mouth and snatched the burned up cigarette into its gullet. Then it continued swimming, just as content as it had always been.

"Goddamn chucklehead," he said.

Smoke on the Wind

Melvin McCoy had never shot at a person before last night. He'd been in a fair share of fist fights throughout his life, but he'd never had to draw a gun on anyone, much less fire it. It was more exciting than he'd expected. As he sat at the end of his driveway, watching the empty country road in front of him, he thought of a song. His left hand tapped out a rhythm on the stock of the gun, and the fingers on his right hand formed chord structures. He sang into the empty and humid morning.

"We gonna romp and tromp till midnight. We gonna fuss and fight till daylight."

As he sang, he picked out a pine needle from the water dish at his feet. He wanted to keep it as fresh as possible. Even though he'd seen that dog drink from a rain puddle, there was no reason not to be presentable. He whistled toward the road, then again into the woods, pausing to listen for a response or the sound of leaves shuffling or a branch swaying. But there were no such sounds. Only the echo of his whistle and the cicadas buzzing around him.

The two boys had come in the early morning hours, before the sun had risen. When he heard the car crunching up his gravel drive, he shot out of bed and grabbed his gun while his dog followed. He peered out the window and saw two boys climb out of a Pontiac sedan. One boy carried a glass bottle. They crept along the edge of his property until they reached the marijuana crop behind his house. Sometimes kids snuck onto his property with knives and machetes, trying to harvest his pot plants. But these boys moved quickly, lightly stepping across the leaves and twigs, making as little noise as possible. They stood on the outside of the crop and tore off buds, shoving them in their pockets, whispering to each other. Normally, he would've loosed his dog after them, but Melvin felt something was about to happen, something he should be prepared for. After a few seconds, the taller boy lit the rag tucked into the bottle. Melvin, without hesitation, fired a shot through his back window.

The bottle exploded in brilliant oranges and yellows. The boy dropped below the plants and rolled to put out the fire crawling up his arm. The second boy ran to the Pontiac and produced another bottle. He lit the rag, and Melvin fired another shot. The second bottle burst, and the flames leapt into the sedan. The taller boy and his friend both ran into the woods.

Melvin rushed outside in his pajamas. Smoke billowed upward from the edge of his crop, dusting the night sky with gray and white. He flew past the sedan, now fully ablaze, and stomped out the fire in his plants. There was no sign of either boy, only the burning Pontiac and broken glass that glittered orange in the raging firelight.

Once the excitement and the fire subsided, he couldn't find his dog anywhere. He whistled throughout the night and trekked into the woods, never straying far from his house. There was no sign of the dog and no sign of the boys. Melvin returned, and sat in a lawn chair on his porch, watching the car burn and burn until the fire finally died. He had stayed up all night waiting for his dog to return.

Sitting in the morning sun, Melvin listened to the birds bouncing from branch to branch in the old oak tree, singing in tones both low and high. He decided to join them.

"We gonna to break out all of the windows. We gonna kick down all the doors. We gonna pitch a wang dang doodle all night long."

Somehow the birds and Howlin' Wolf all came together like a church choir, Melvin and the birds singing beside the cannabis plants. Off to the side, in a charred circle of grass, sat the burned out Pontiac sedan. The metal was charred to a deep black, and the tires were dried puddles of rubber, pooled beneath the wheels. Melvin considered whether or not his business was worth the carnage. Was it worth his life? Was there something else he could do to make money? He thought about the boy with the flaming arm and then laughed.

"Brought whiskey to a gunfight," he said into the open air.

His business was volatile, dangerous, and illegal. But it was his business. These boys had tried to burn his crop, and he, Melvin McCoy, had fought them off. This was his house. This was his business. That was his dog. They could all go to hell.

~

Max and Rosie stood on the side of the road and watched as the smoke from their car's engine began to die down. Everything that was in the trunk was now piled in the grass. They were afraid that the car might catch fire. Max paced back and forth, and Rosie sat on the grass and stared at the desolate stretch of road in front of them. They hadn't seen another car since they crossed into South Carolina over an hour ago. She was nine weeks pregnant.

They had been driving for almost two hundred miles when the engine in their car gave out somewhere between Eutawville and Moncks Corner in South Carolina. While speeding down the back roads of Berkeley County, Max had noticed an unusual amount of smoke rising from underneath the hood of the 1977 Chevrolet Vega. The smoke had not alarmed him as much as the clanking sound that soon followed.

"Did you change the oil before we left?" Rosie asked.

"Oil change won't fix a fifty-year-old car." He gave the fender a hard kick, tearing some of the rust.

"Just sit down. Someone will come." She shielded her eyes from the sun.

The weather report on the radio had said the temperature would break 100. Max would've guessed it was closer to 115. The smoke and heat from the car only added to the sweat coursing down his back, sticking to his shirt. Even the shade of the large pines along the roadside wasn't enough relief. There was no breeze. In either direction, the road was empty, a solitary stretch of pavement that began and ended upon the horizon. Max felt for a moment, as if he and Rosie were the last two people on Earth. "There's nobody around," he said.

She did not reply. The engine smoke was carried upward by a warm wind that blew down the empty bronze-colored road. Max started digging through his bag and found a pack of Camels and a lighter.

"I thought you said you would quit," Rosie said.

He lit the tip of the cigarette and took a long drag. "I didn't say when." He blew the smoke into the sky.

"It's bad for the baby," she said.

Max shuffled farther away from her and sat down in the grass. Rosie had insisted on coming through the back roads because she was scared of everything, though she wouldn't admit it. She was scared of everything since she found out she was pregnant, scared of the exhaust fumes, the sleepy truck drivers, the angry commuters paying more attention to email than to other cars. And Max wanted to make her happy. He had agreed to go to her sister's place in Charleston for the weekend. He'd even agreed to take the "back way" for more fresh air. Now, they were stuck, their only clue as to their whereabouts being a twisted road sign a few miles back that read "Berkeley County Line."

He glanced over at Rosie, still lying on the grass. She'll be sunburned before too long, he thought. Rosie's red hair mingled in the dead grass, picking up small bits of dirt and leaves. She didn't seem to mind. "It's always bad for the baby," he said.

"We have to make changes now."

"We have enough change on our own. Do we really need another one?"

"Don't start that," she said.

"I was trying to be helpful." He paused, unsure if he should continue. After a moment he said, "It's a simple procedure."

Rosie lifted her shirt, exposing the subtle curve of her stomach to the sun, as if to taunt him with the reality of what he had suggested. She opened one eye to look at him, then turned away. "It's not a discussion," she said.

Max opened his mouth to reply, but the words didn't come to him. He wiped a trickle of sweat from his temple, then flicked his used cigarette onto the road.

For a minute neither of the pair spoke a word. The birds overhead sang low warbling songs, the whistles and chirps and calls blended into one off-key chorus. Max lay his head in the crispy grass, facing Rosie who lay on her back with one hand on her swollen stomach. Since Rosie had found out she was pregnant, everything between them had become complicated beyond what Max had expected. He loved her; he knew that. But the idea of being a father at this point in his life made his stomach clench. There were things he needed to do, and even with Rosie as the mother, a child would mean the end of those things. He thought about their trip to see her sister in Charleston, and Max was now unsure if both of them would return home.

"I'm sorry about what I said," he said.

"I'm sure you are," she said.

As Max got up, the wind carried a faint clanging noise down the road. He squinted in the direction of the sound but couldn't see anything. "Do you hear that noise?" he asked Rosie.

"What noise?"

"Listen."

Some ways down the road, a small outline bobbed up and down, moving towards them. Max squinted to see further down the road as the figure jingled along.

"It's a dog," he said with some confusion.

A brown and white lab mix trotted to the couple until he was just a few feet away. He gave a shrill bark, as if he hadn't spoken to anyone for some time.

Max whistled.

"What if he's got rabies or something?" Rosie was sitting up now.

"He's got a collar, so he's got an owner. And he's not foaming." Max whistled again, but the dog sat down in the middle of the lane and stared at them, it's tail shifting back and forth. Max walked up to the dog and patted its head. The dog seemed pleased. On its collar tag was scratched: "Property of The Voodoo Man." Max read the engraving aloud then looked back at Rosie who was now standing behind him. Neither of them said anything for a moment. Finally Rosie spoke.

"He smells like smoke," she said, keeping her distance.

Max smelled the dog's fur. He smelt like a campfire.

"Is he hurt?"

"I don't think so." Max looked up the empty road. He and Rosie had been waiting for almost an hour in the heat, and he knew they couldn't take much more. He stood up and started walking up the bronze colored pavement in the direction the dog had come. Max whistled and the lab mix followed suit. Rosie stood behind them.

"Where are you going?"

Max stopped. "To find the dog's owner so we can call someone to get the hell out of here."

"You're walking?"

Max took off his shoes and handed them to Rosie. "Put these on."

Rosie slipped off her sandals and put Max's shoes on. She half-smiled. "What'll you wear?"

Max looked at the dog, wagging his tail.

"He made it fine with no shoes."

~

Max, Rosie, and the dog came through the thick line of trees separating the driveway from the main road. They, and the dog in tow, pushed their way through the trees. When they came into the yard, the dog ran off toward a man sitting in a chair with a gun. Max stopped at the edge of the yard, putting a hand across Rosie's shoulder and called out to the man.

"Excuse me," he said. Rosie shook under his hand, her skin wet from the heat.

The man stood up and walked across the small yard toward the couple. He was a small framed black man, and as he walked to them, he pulled his hat down to cover the tops of his eyes. A sedan, black with soot and smoke above the windows, sat underneath a tree in puddles of melted rubber. As the man walked down the driveway, still carrying his rifle, Max caught the scent of fire and smoke, and something else that took him a moment to place. It was a smell that brought him back to high school, to the dingy bathrooms between classes, to late nights after football games. When he placed the smell of marijuana, he regretted that he and Rosie had found this man. The oily and earthy smell crept along with the man as he made his way toward them. Max could taste it in his mouth.

"What?" the man asked, his voice rough and scratchy.

Max stammered a response as two wrens warbled and bounced in the tree behind the man.

"You got one more chance to get it out or I'll pull it out of you myself."

Rosie said, "Our car broke down and we need a phone to call someone to come get us."

"How far?" When neither responded he re-emphasized the question. "How far are you from here?"

"The car is a half mile up the road, going north," she said.

"You need to get on." The man kept looking past Max and Rosie, as if he were expecting something to come from the trees.

Rosie spoke up again, pleading in her voice. "Please, we'll only be just a minute. I'd really like to get off my feet for a bit too."

Max wasn't sure what the man would do. He kept his grip on the rifle in his hand and studied them very intently. The man's eyes lingered over Rosie.

"You pregnant, girlie?"

The couple swapped surprised looks. Max could hear his heart, now growing louder than the birds overhead. The man suddenly seemed proud of himself.

"It's a gift."

"So can you help us?"

The man looked through the trees again. "You got five minutes. You give them this address, I cut the line and you can walk the fifty miles to Charleston."

The man spat on the ground and Max's head was starting to swim from the smell that seemed to have made its home in everything around them. It followed the man like a specter, as if it were a part of him. He wondered what he had gotten Rosie into. They followed the man, past the sickly sweet stink of the marijuana, past the burned out Pontiac, and into the front door of his small ranch house.

~

It had occurred to Melvin that the couple might be part of the same gang terrorizing him, but the notion slipped past when he realized she was pregnant. She wasn't showing much, but he could see it in her eyes, something he learned from his mother. She'd always said that when women get to being with child, they carry themselves differently and have a different look in their eye, a searching for some place to call home.

As he led the couple into his house, he became keenly aware of the things that were around him. With the dog in front of him, Melvin muttered a half-apology to the couple for the mess. He picked up a Gibson Dot guitar lying on the carpet and set it back in the decorative case, the case on which he, in his earlier and more revolutionary days, had painted a colorful and psychedelic 'Voodoo Man' across the hard plastic surface. The name had been given to him back then because of his dark skin and the songs he made the Gibson sing. It became something else entirely when he started growing and selling pot. That career change hadn't been a choice as he saw it, but a lack of options. It had been, and still was, the only way he could earn.

The dog beside him licked his cheek. With his friend at his side, Melvin forgot about the boys who had attacked him last night, and that they might return any time.

The couple was staring at him, and he snapped back to the present.

"Names," he said.

"I'm Max and this is Rosie." The boy gestured at the girl. "We didn't get your name."

"I didn't give it to you. Phone's in here. You got five minutes."

Melvin stood behind the boy while he called a truck to come and get them. At first, Melvin fidgeted with the phone line that ran into the wall, ready to pull it out. But as the conversation continued, Melvin found himself glancing back at Rosie, sitting on the couch across the room. She had shoulder-length red hair and paper-white skin. There was a lightness to her, an unmistakable optimism that she carried in her face, the kind only a woman with child has. The boy, however, carried a weariness in his shoulders, a heavy load that the man recognized immediately for its familiarity. He hadn't been listening to the boy's call. Max finally hung up.

"Said they can be at the car in an hour. Thanks for your help. We'll leave you be now."

Melvin hesitated a moment, then surprised himself. "If you need to wash up a little, you can use the hall bath."

Rosie perked up at the idea, and Melvin showed her the bathroom and how to operate the toilet so that it wouldn't overflow. Rosie closed the door and Melvin sat on a dusty vinyl sofa and the dog lay down by his feet. Max still stood in the hallway by the phone, then slunked to a chair opposite Melvin. The two sat in silence for a few seconds, Max trying to hide the tremors in his hands.

Melvin laughed. "I ain't gonna kill you."

"You're not afraid of us telling someone about the pot in your backyard?"

"Should I be?" Melvin asked with a feigned seriousness. He could hear Rosie moving in the bathroom, the old floor flexing under her feet.

"No, sir," Max said, a crack in his voice.

Melvin laughed again at having ribbed the boy. "Relax. I bet you don't even know where you are."

"How did you start doing all that?" he asked, motioning outside.

Melvin paused again, taking his time. The thought of honesty had made him nervous in the past, made his hands sweat. But they were dry now.

"When I was about your age, I used to play solo gigs, one bar to the next," he pointed at the Gibson in the corner. "When that never got big, I planted me a crop and," he motioned outside, "all that."

The two sat listening to the sounds of running water coming down the hall from the bathroom. Melvin took a long breath and decided to jump into what was bothering him.

"Is she carrying your baby?"

There was more silence. The room was growing hotter and Melvin could see the shine of sweat coming into Max's face. He saw the undersides of the boy's toes were worn red from walking with no shoes. Melvin was surprised he had missed it. The boy licked his lips and crossed his arms. "Yes, sir."

Melvin kept watching the boy's toes rolling across the floor, his skin red and pink with the beginnings of blisters on a few of the toes. The boy's skin hadn't been prepared for such a harsh road in such harsh heat. Melvin thought about the aged brown carpet coming up along the edges and the yellowed drywall, how everything around him was infused with this way of living, but here in front of him sat this boy, untouched by the chaos around them and unaware of what Melvin knew might come down the driveway at any moment.

"You only get one shot at being a good father," Melvin said. "You botch that, it's over. My daddy left when I was still sucking at the tit. Left me and my mom living out of cars and getting dressed for school in public bathrooms. But you don't care about that none. You ain't worthless like my daddy was, judging how you give your shoes to your girl." He watched as Max acknowledged his own bare feet with a glance. "I ain't pretending to have some kind of magic whatnot for you," he said. "But the good book says life is like a smoke, or a mist, or something like that. It's here," he snapped his fingers. "Then it's gone. That's it." He paused for a moment. "That's what I got to say about that."

The older man leaned back into the couch as the dog rolled over onto his boots. He reached down and rubbed the dog's stomach. Max continued staring at his feet and finally took a deep breath.

"I appreciate everything you've done for us, sir. But, with all due respect, Rosie and I—"

He cut Max off with a wave of his hand as the dog's head snapped up and looked toward the front yard. The dog got up and began sniffing around the front window, all around the wood paneling and the broken floor vents. Rosie came down the hallway, her face brighter and her hair a little less dusty.

"What's going on?" she asked with a smile.

Melvin got up and grabbed his gun from the foyer and looked through the blinds. He stood still for a moment. The dog turned and looked back at him. Melvin squatted down and gave the dog one last scratch behind his ears then leashed the dog's collar and handed it to the boy. The dog whimpered again as the sound of tires on gravel rolled into the house.

"What're you doing?" Max asked, leash in hand.

Melvin turned and looked at the couple, both wearing looks of amazement and confusion. The girl in her yellow dress and the boy in his plaid button-up, grasping onto the dog's leash with both hands. He wondered where he had put the old Polaroid camera from years back. The moment seemed to be one that deserved a picture or at least some sort of keepsake to remember what had happened. All at once, the sound of slamming car doors and the boy holding his dog and the girl's hair, more orange than red in the sunlight, caught up with him and he became overwhelmed with the thought that this could be the last pleasant moment of his life.

Melvin McCoy looked the boy over once. He took a heavy breath and said to Max, "I need you to take care of that dog for me."

~

Melvin stared out the window and watched as three men exited a beige sedan. Actually, it was one man and two boys. He recognized those two boys from last night. The taller one had his arm wrapped up in a makeshift bandage, and both he and the other boy wore deep scratches on their faces and arms. The man with them, a small gangly white fellow, hollered for him to come out peaceably. Melvin had already sent the couple out the back door with his dog. He was going to miss that dog.

Melvin gripped his rifle and stepped out onto the front landing. The man smiled when he saw him. He wore a black t-shirt and ratty jeans and sunglasses. The left lens was tinted pitch black, while the right was mirrored. One lens shimmered, bouncing the light in all directions while the other drank in every bit of light it could.

"Don't believe I know you," Melvin said.

The man smiled. The light glistened off the one mirrored lens. "Good morning, Mr. McCoy," he said. "My name is Jackson Matte. I'm glad to finally meet you in person."

"I see you left the whiskey at home," Melvin said.

Jackson smiled and shook his head. "I'm afraid these boys misunderstood my directions." He clapped the taller one hard on the back. The boy stumbled forward. "A nice big plot of weed like you got ain't no use to me all burned up. But you know what they say. If you want something done right and all that." He sounded bored, as if he'd done this two or three times already today. Melvin and Jackson stood in silence for a moment until Jackson motioned the boys toward Melvin's house. They seemed frightened, as if disobeying him or coming against Melvin would have the same outcome. The boys came forward, then waited. Melvin stepped down into the yard, now even with Jackson. The boys ran past him into the house.

"What if I call the sheriff?" Melvin asked with a smile.

Jackson laughed. He took off his sunglasses and cleaned the black lens on his dirty t-shirt. The sun glinted off a revolver tucked into his jeans. "Those bottles last night was meant for your house, not your plot. Think of it as a retirement party, old man." He put the glasses back on and pulled the revolver from his waistband, as casual as could be.

Melvin scoffed and watched as Jackson put his glasses back on his face and spat on the ground. The boys were throwing furniture down on the floor, making a mess of things. They started a fire in his living room. Melvin stood as still as he could, the flames growing at his back. He had decided, in that instant, not to kill this man, Jackson. He saw himself put down his gun and walk away from all of it. He envisioned a small place near town in which to settle into an acceptable routine. People his age usually worked in grocery stores. That wouldn't be all bad, he thought. Maybe he could find a woman who wouldn't hate him like so many others had. He had decided that he would finally give it all up when he felt the first bullet enter his chest.

His brain moved through memories like a film reel on fast forward. Images of his father and the dog and the couple and Rosie's yellow dress and her red hair and the baby that would come after. It would be a girl, he thought. His mother had always known how to predict such things and he had the gift as well. He could predict such things as surely as someone could watch a tower of clouds gathering in the sky and say that it's going to rain. He felt his body quiver from a second bullet, and he fell down on the porch. He thought about his dog again, and he hoped Max and Rosie's child would love that dog. They should give it a fitting name, he thought. He'd never been good with names, never could seem to find the right fit for anything in his life. It seemed like such a dishonor to waste a mediocre name on such a wonderful dog. He realized he never taught them that Howlin' Wolf song before they left. That baby should know good music, real tunes and feeling. That slow feeling, that explosive feeling. The fire behind him roared to life, and Melvin McCoy shut his eyes and went to sleep.

~

Max wasn't given time to understand exactly what the man had meant when he handed the leash to him. He had hurried them out the back door and Max and Rosie had both stopped when they saw the crop of marijuana. He, Rosie, and the dog ran through the waist high plants, kicking over stalks and bending the green cannabis fingers as they went. That skunk smell latched onto their clothes and followed them into the woods that surrounded the back of the house.

They ran through the small clearing and into a patch of trees behind the house. Max tried to be as quiet as possible, but his bare feet were bleeding and he wanted to scream. He motioned to Rosie to lie still and keep the dog quiet. Past the plot of bright green cannabis, he heard the muffled voices rising on the wind. The birds overhead were drowning out anything more. The stinking smell of marijuana that latched itself so firmly to the dog earlier seemed to be dissipating now.

The voices grew quiet, and Max heard two loud pops that he knew were gunshots. His breathing seemed louder than the world around him. He saw Rosie holding onto the dog's neck and covering her mouth with her hand. The dog fought against her, trying to run back through the woods to the house. Max wrapped his arms around it and held on.

They sat still for another minute until a tower of black smoke rose over them. After a minute, flames burned through the windows of the house and two boys and another man set to uprooting the drug crop in the back yard. Max knew they had to wait for the men to leave before he and Rosie and the dog could find a way out. The things he'd said earlier in the day seemed so long ago, days and days past. He didn't know what they would do next, how they would get out of this place and back to their own world. The smell of fire and carnage crept through the woods, and he knew that in the heat of the day, it would make its way up to them, but his eyes were fixed on the smoke that went higher and higher until it disappeared into the white clouds. Max placed his hand on the solid, subtle curve of Rosie's midsection.

Tongues of Fire

Momma said the church burnt down in '85, the same day I was born. Said it was on account of someone leaving a space heater running overnight in the sanctuary. Close as anyone could figure, it got too close to a pew cushion. She never told me who it was what left the heater on, but I think she knew. Most said it was Randy Lyons' boy, Cedric. He was touched in the head, real forgetful and affectionate. He hugged everybody he saw and never had no sense of boundaries. During a potluck fellowship, he cornered Charlotte Holbrooke in a Sunday school room, kept telling her how pretty she was and gave her a big hug. He hugged her so hard she screamed, but Cedric wouldn't let her go. Her daddy run in and knocked the two of 'em down, started hitting on poor Cedric. The boy didn't mean no harm, but Mr. Holbrooke said that wasn't no good excuse. He wanted Cedric beat in front of the whole church for hurting his girl. Nobody figured that was fit. The church wasn't up for beating a boy as touched as Cedric.

Momma always said the Holy Spirit visited the church so often they had him a seat saved up front. People was always shouting and speaking in tongues and laying on hands. They used to say the Holy Spirit was fire from heaven, come to cleanse us for Jesus. A year before I was born, a travelling preacher showed up carrying a metal box with a key lock and holes poked all in it. He preached that Sunday about the hand of God protecting his children, that we was sheltered beneath his wing. He unlocked that box in the pulpit and pulled out the biggest rattlesnake Momma ever saw, even to this day. That man shouted and called upon the Lord to protect him, to test his faith. That snake got to wiggling and the preacher dropped it right on Pearl Jenkins lap in the front row. She stood up, shouted, then passed out. Charlotte Holbrooke's daddy run to her and threw his coat over her legs so old Pearl didn't show no one her glory. When he did, he stepped right on that rattler's tail and the daggum thing bit him on the ankle. We thought he'd be dead for sure. Turned out that preacher'd been milking his snakes just in case God decided he hadn't been faithful enough. Mr. Holbrooke said the place was a freak show, started calling down curse after curse on families and preachers and animals alike. We never saw him again, and no one ever called on the snake preacher either. Most everyone figured that the Lord gave us the common sense enough not to pick up such a creature. That seemed protection enough not to get bit.

A year after that, Momma went into labor with me. She brought a midwife with her to the hospital, to honor the old ways, she says. The midwife was old school Pentecostal. While the doctors went to work, she stood over Momma, laid hands on her, and prayed in tongues for near about a hour. Momma said when she looked at the midwife, she was wearing a crown of fire, though the doctors say it was probably the drugs working on her. Apparently, it was a very cleansing experience.

Out where the church used to be, there ain't hardly nothing now. Structure caved in and brought the steeple down with it. Momma says the steeple came down the same moment I opened my eyes into the world, as that midwife was praying in tongues. Ain't no way to prove that, but it's a neat thought. The mess of a church is outside the city limit, so it's up to the county to clean it up. They don't seem to be in no rush seeing as it's been almost twenty years. The building's scattered but the fire never touched the graveyard out behind the building. So now there's a pile of charred lumber spread in front of the most pristine graveyard you ever seen. Momma said there was such a spirit in that church, like the apostles on the day of Pentecost with their tongues of flame. Anyone who watched that building burn down on the night I was born would probably agree with her.

Flood Lines

The mall had sat abandoned for three weeks. When Hurricane Josephine had come through and flooded half of Berkeley County, the shopping mall, sitting in a low-lying plot of land, had been the first to be found underwater. Half of the store windows had been crushed by the weight of the water and forest debris. Even from a distance, passersby could make out a perfectly straight line stained into the brick from where the flood waters had once sat, unmoving for nearly two weeks.

It had been Sam's idea to break in through the loading dock, and Bailey had followed along as she always did. The two girls had known each other since the first day of kindergarten. They began their time as rivals, Sam the daughter of strict Filipino immigrants, and Bailey's father a local pastor with expectations as high as heaven. As they grew older, they found a kindred spirit in each other and eventually became friends. Sam had likened it to prisoners of war who bond over shared trauma and torture.

The doors, once the back entrance to a 99 cents fashion store, were chained together, held tight by a rusted padlock. By now, the flood waters had soaked into the clay soil beneath the foundation. Bailey wondered if all that water had found its way into the ground water supply. In science class, Mr. Thornton had told them about aquifers, underground rivers that ran for hundreds of miles under their feet. "This county," he'd said, sipping from his large thermos, "is home to several underground rivers."

He'd smirked as if this fact had changed his students' lives, then rubbed his perfectly round midsection.

The brick wall bore the same water line as the rest of the structure. Everything above sun-bleached and everything below green with algae and pond scum. Bailey stood next to it, using her hand to measure her height against the discolored line.

Sam shook the chain and lock wrapped around the door's handles. "You bring your dad's cutters?"

Bailey unzipped her backpack and handed the tool to Sam. Growing up in her dad's small country churches, most of her friends had been the same type of person: well-dressed, well-mannered church kids whose parents wanted an "in" with the pastor. Her mother praised the church girls' dresses and willingness to serve the Lord by passing out bulletins or reading a scripture on Sunday. Her father nodded in approval at the children's choir singing "Great is Thy Faithfulness" and other holy hymns. They had not approved of her friendship with Sam.

They knew of Samantha Alcantara, like everyone else in their small part of the county. But they knew the Sam Alcantara who smoked behind the movie theater and threw balloons filled with paint at passing cars. But no one knew the Sam that Bailey knew, the witty, ferocious, and fearless Sam who stood up to bullies and mean girls, the Sam who once broke into the announcer's booth during a basketball game and let loose a fury of curses and crude jokes while parents gasped and their children cackled with laughter. Two male administrators had to kick the door open and drag her away from the microphone.

Bailey had been at the game, blushing while sitting next to her parents, who did not gasp or shame her secret friend like the others. Instead, they wore looks of deep sorrow and pity for the girl who felt so unseen that she resorted to antics like this for attention. Bailey wondered what bible verses were running through their heads, or if this story would show up in one of her father's fiery sermons.

Sam leveraged her entire body against the cutters. After a few grunts and curses, she broke through the steel chain, and it clattered to the concrete. She passed the cutters back to Bailey, and the two girls heaved open the steel doors.

The air inside rushed into their faces, a wind carrying rot and decay and rust.

"Great day," Bailey said, tucking her face into her t-shirt.

Sam laughed. "We gotta get you cursing like a real person."

Bailey laughed too. She had only cursed twice in her life. The first was as a child, trying to find a word to rhyme with "truck." Her parents had gently corrected her and explained the danger of that word. The second time had been when she broke her toe playing volleyball at a church function. That same word from her childhood spilled from her mouth as those good church folks froze from shock. Her parents had been less gentle in their correction that time.

"I'm just not that creative," Bailey said, shielding her nose from the smell still pouring through the doorway. Of course, she was lying. She didn't curse because she knew that God didn't approve of it. And He was always watching. Even now she imagined him peering through the open doors as the two girls crossed into the abandoned store.

"Troy said the pet store is towards the other end," Sam said. She clicked on a flashlight.

"I thought we were just here so you could tag a wall or something."

Sam laughed again. "We are," she said, shaking the spray cans in her bag. "But he said there's like a pack of wild dogs and birds living here now. They couldn't get all the animals out of the pet store in time, so they went feral."

Bailey pictured a group of puppies, teeth bared, fur raised, encircling them. The thought made her laugh.

The two girls walked through the store, littered with overturned displays, mannequins, and piles of moldy clothes.

"It's toxic in here," Bailey said. Now both girls had their t-shirts pulled up over their mouths and noses. With her face covered, Bailey could only see Sam's eyes. Even in the dark, they caught what little light there was. Bailey could see, maybe for the first time, she thought, that they were brown, the deep brown of rich wood. She gave her friend a thumbs up then pulled her hair up, tying it tight and trying not to think about what garbage or filth might be under their feet.

The only light in the whole mall streamed in from the ceiling through the massive skylights that lit the spaces between the stores. They made their way through the broken display window and into the main walkway. In the half-dark, the mall seemed to stretch forever in every direction, only the faint afternoon light giving any indication of its true size.

"Which way?" Bailey asked.

Sam motioned towards a large fountain and they made their way to it.

"I remember this," Sam said. "My parents used to let me throw pennies in here."

Bailey didn't know what to say. Since coming out to them, Sam rarely talked about her parents. Though no one but Sam really knew, rumors ran through their school that her parents had kicked her out of the house, that her father had hit her, and her mother had disowned her. Others said that Sam had emancipated herself from them and was living with relatives in Eutawville. Bailey had tried to stay out of the flow of gossip, but it washed over her nonetheless.

"What did you wish for?" Bailey asked. "When they let you throw pennies in."

Sam, without hesitation, said, "a new family."

Bailey unzipped her bag and started digging. She found two paperclips and handed them to Sam and said, "I don't have any coins."

Sam smiled. "You're such a fucking loser," she said, then took one of the paperclips and flung it into the stale brown water. She hitched up her bag and walked deeper into the mall. Bailey stood for a moment, unsure of what to wish for. Her parents had taught her wishes were useless, that only prayers made any difference in the circumstances of life. And so, without a wish of her own, she made a wish for her friend, and tossed her paperclip into the murky fountain.

~

The weather man on TV had rolled up his shirt sleeves. That's how everyone in the county knew this hurricane would be serious. Growing up in the low country of South Carolina, Bailey had weathered at least ten hurricanes and tropical storms. But when the meteorologist stepped onto their TV screen, no blazer and sleeves rolled up to his elbows, they knew this storm would be different.

Hurricane Josephine had torn through the Charleston peninsula, drowning the swanky downtown condos and shotgun houses in surging storm water. But the eye wall barreled into the northern counties, pushing the lakes above their banks and hurling pines through houses and rearranging the landscape as it saw fit.

The mall had been the first casualty. As the skies cleared and the storm broke apart, looky-loos started wandering around the county to see what roads were washed out and which homes had suffered the worst. Before long, a crowd of people gathered at the mall, Bailey and her parents among them. It reminded her of the prayer circles in church, and she wondered if her father would say a prayer for everyone.

"I hope everyone got out okay," someone next to them said.

Her father sighed. "Like the days of Noah. The Lord lays waste to the wicked earth." Her mother followed it with a quiet amen. Bailey pretended to know what her father meant and so she nodded her head.

A few yards away she saw Sam's parents, arms crossed and looking more sad than the rest of the onlookers. Mrs. Alcantara leaned against her husband and began to cry and Bailey was a touch embarrassed for them.

~

The two girls made their way down the sunlit corridors, past shop windows, some shattered and some flexed from the pressure of the flood waters. Store after store, Sam and Bailey explored the old scattered clothes and mildewed wares.

"Feels like the end of the world," Bailey said.

"It's great isn't it?"

Bailey laughed. The two of them wandered through a sporting goods store. Sam picked up a wooden bat and motioned towards her friend. Bailey smiled and grabbed a ball from the shelf and wound up like she'd seen pitchers do on TV. She threw the ball and Sam swung, making contact. The bat was so water-logged that the ball simply dropped at her feet with a wet slap. Both girls laughed, then changed positions. Bailey swung at the pitch and made contact. This time, the ball soared into the plate glass window at the front of the store, leaving a white mark from the impact.

Sam grinned, and even in the dark, Bailey could see the devious smile on her friend's face. Sam picked up another ball and heaved it at the window. The glass flexed and groaned.

"No one's watching," Sam said, and tossed another ball to Bailey.

Bailey held the ball for a moment. Jesus was watching, she knew. She imagined him peering into the window, hands cupped around his eyes, wagging his finger. Bailey reared her arm back and threw the ball with every bit of strength she had.

The glass shattered, spilling shards into the empty mall. Sam cheered.

"Fuck yeah," she yelled and hugged Bailey, picking her up like at the end of a winning game. Sam's hands were bigger than Bailey had realized, wrapping her sides and back in a way she'd never felt before.

Sam set her down, grinning like an idiot. "Feels good to be a Jezebel, doesn't it?"

Both girls stuffed their bags with as many balls as they could, rushed out into the corridor, and started throwing.

No window or display was safe. The girls hurled balls and sticks and whatever else the flood had left behind in every direction. Bailey ripped a map display out of its case and rolled it up, tucking it into her bag. Sam pulled a bone knife from her bag and carved her name into the soft wood of a park bench. Bailey admired the knife.

"Where'd you get that?"

"The lake spit it up," Sam said, finishing her inscription. "Washed ashore one day."

"My parents would never let me have a knife," Bailey said.

Sam scoffed and jabbed the knife deeper into the seat of the bench. She carved in silence, focused and determined.

Bailey decided this was her moment.

"Everyone at school talks about you," she said.

"Fuck 'em."

"Hailey said your parents hit you and kicked you out. When you. You know…"

Sam kept carving. "Then Hailey's a liar *and* a cunt," she said.

Bailey surprised herself by giggling. The more time she spent around Sam the more she grew accustomed to hearing language that her parents would weep over.

"You can tell me," Bailey said. She didn't know if she should touch her friend or not even though something warm inside her was begging her to.

Sam grew silent for a long time, just carving. No longer writing anything but digging as deep as she could into the bench. Finally, she turned and stared at Bailey.

"Then you're a cunt too," she said, getting up and throwing the knife into her backpack.

"You don't mean that," Bailey said, biting back some small sadness.

Sam sighed. "Yeah, I don't," she said.

The girls walked together down the mall corridor in silence. The sunlight that stabbed through the skylight openings reminded Bailey of all the paintings of heaven that hung in her parents' church. The dust and spores that floated through the air gave each beam a direct path, a purpose for existence even.

"I'm sorry I asked," Bailey said.

Sam continued in silence.

"What's it like being a lesbian?" she asked, though she wasn't sure why.

Sam laughed. "Why don't you ask the lesbians in your church?"

"We don't have any."

"Your dad would freak if he knew."

Bailey's chest tightened and her skin bristled.

"They're everywhere," Sam said, waving her hands about as if she were talking about aliens or body snatchers. She laughed. "Besides," she said, "Everybody's a little bit gay."

"Dad says it's a sin."

"Like old lady Reeve's gossip or the 'coffee' that Mr. Thornton keeps in his cup during class?"

Bailey frowned. "It's different though. That's what he says."

Sam let out a frustrated sigh. "What do you say?"

Bailey didn't answer, and Sam sighed, shifting her bag and rattling the spray cans inside. "Come on," she said. "Let's find that pet store."

~

"We don't want you hanging out with Sam anymore."

Twilight glimmered along the horizon as Bailey and her parents locked up the front doors of the church. They walked in a tidy row towards the parsonage where they lived. Another Wednesday night bible study finished and, walking through the gravel lot, past the makeshift homes and tennements scattered along the lake shore, Bailey's parents echoed their sentiment, more sure and steady than before.

"We've heard the stories about her, and we're worried she might lead you astray," her mother said.

"She's not helping you grow in your walk with Christ," her father added in his most pastoral voice. His arms were crossed over his chest as if he didn't know how else to hold them.

Bailey spoke quickly. "I'm trying to help her. She's lost."

Her mother touched Bailey's tangled red hair. "We're proud of you for that," she said. "But we don't think you're mature enough to help her find her faith without risking your own."

Something snapped in Bailey's chest. For fifteen years she had done everything they'd asked. Every weekend, revivals and Sunday school and service. Every Wednesday, bible studies and prayer meetings. Every summer, youth group camp and retreats. All of it was fine. She even enjoyed parts of it. The songs, hearing the old folks' stories and gossip disguised as prayer requests, even the freedom that came with the summer camps. But, for some reason that she couldn't find, or didn't want to, this was too much.

"Sam gets me," she said, louder than she'd intended. "She's nice and doesn't treat me like the other kids do."

"How do the other kids treat you?" her mother asked.

Bailey hesitated, then said, "like a pastor's kid."

Something in her response wounded her father. He exhaled and, even in the rising dark, Bailey could see the hurt in his face. "We want what's best for your soul," he said.

"Do you want her to go to hell?" Bailey snapped.

"That is unfair," her mother said. "We all make our own choices."

"Why can't I make my own?" Bailey said.

Her father said, "The Lord has charged us with protecting you and shepherding your soul."

"Then who is gonna shepherd Sam's soul?"

All three fell silent, Bailey busying her mind by counting each footstep that crunched through the gravel lot.

~

The mall was more of a labyrinth than Bailey had remembered. Maybe it was the dimly lit store fronts, the wrecked signs that dangled from each one, the broken windows, but she had no idea where they were. Like every other kid in their area, she'd spend hours wandering the mall on the weekends, mostly with her parents. But now, stalking among the silent and empty corridors, Bailey felt as if she and Sam were the only people left in the world, two survivors bound and clung together among the wreckage that surrounded them.

"Feels like the end of the world," Bailey said.

"You already said that," Sam replied.

"But it's all I can think about."

Sam pulled a joint and a lighter out of her pocket. She lit the twisted end and took a long pull.

Bailey pretended not to see. Sam came closer and took another long drag, sending a cascade of skunky smoke into the humid air around them.

"You shouldn't be doing that," Bailey said.

Sam laughed. "You gonna call the police?"

"No," Bailey said too quickly. "If there's animals or people here they'll smell it."

"I think all the broken windows would've given us away."

Bailey giggled. She didn't know if it was the excitement of being in the abandoned mall, the second hand smoke, or being around Sam again, but her head was spinning.

"Give it here," she said, gesturing to Sam.

"No," Sam said. "I'm not sending the pastor's kid to hell." She laughed.

Bailey snatched the joint from between her friend's lips and inhaled, filling her lungs to their capacity.

She hadn't expected it to burn so much. Every ounce of smoke and air came billowing out of her mouth and nose at the same time, and for a moment Bailey thought she would die. Sam slapped her back until she started coughing and inhaling, looking for some kind of relief. Somewhere in the new fog of her world, Sam was laughing, or someone else was laughing, she couldn't be sure.

"Fucking Virgin Mary over here," Sam said, still laughing.

Bailey tried to laugh or respond but all she could do was cough. After a few seconds, she could breathe again. And after a few more seconds, she said, in a raw and raspy voice, "that was too much."

They laughed together. Two girls sat on the edge of a broken store display and each took another drag, although Bailey inhaled a little less deeply this time.

"Will I get high?" Bailey asked.

"You'll probably throw up," Sam said.

Somehow the prospect of throwing up in an abandoned mall was worse than doing drugs in one.

"Looks like we're both going to hell then," Sam said. She sidled up next to Bailey and the two touched shoulders. Bailey's skin flushed under her t-shirt. This was the most time she had ever spent with Sam, though it had barely been an hour since they met up and walked to the mall. She wondered how she'd been able to call Sam her friend, yet have spent so little time with her.

"That's it," Sam said, staring off into the distance. She walked to a blank brick wall and used her hands to rub the dirt and grime from the surface. No matter how much dirt fell to the ground, the water line remained, the same line that the flood waters had etched along every vertical surface. A testimony to the flood.

Sam opened her bag and dumped a pile of spray cans at her feet. Bailey watched as her friend sprayed line after line, with seemingly no order or plan. She took two more drags from the blunt, and realized she was beginning to enjoy it, the sensation of smoke filling up her lungs. Across the corridor, Sam seemed to be moving in slow motion at times or sped up at others, like a montage in one of those old movies her parents loved to watch. She wondered if she could live in this mall. There was plenty of space. She could sleep in a different store every night. There was a sleeping bag in her parents' garage, and she had plenty of clothes. Here, no one could tell her or Sam what they had to do or couldn't do or couldn't be. She began to imagine other outings or excursions they could have together until she had imagined a new life for both of them, a life without her parents disapproval and without Sam's huddled together and crying. This could be their sanctuary.

She had become so lost in thought, that she hadn't noticed that Sam was finished. Bailey didn't know how much time had passed, though she knew it couldn't be more than a few minutes. But even those minutes seemed like an eternity to her now. She focused her shaky eyesight to the wall across from her where Sam stood, gazing at her spray painted creation. Stretched along the bare brick wall was a mural, a field of wildflowers dotted with butterflies and streaked with sunshine. Along the flood line, Sam had painted the horizon, that testimony of the flood's destruction now sprouting with green grass and flowers.

Bailey walked to the mural and stood next to her friend.

"It's beautiful," she said.

"It's shit," Sam said. "Couldn't get the proportions on the petals right."

The two girls stood, staring at the mural, breathing in the paint fumes and residual weed smoke.

"My parents didn't say anything," Sam said. "When I came out. They just looked so sad, and my dad left the room. My mom just kept on knitting, like nothing had ever happened. They never even brought it up again, even now."

Bailey didn't know whether it was the weed, the paint fumes, or her own feelings, but she asked, "Would you rather they'd thrown you out?"

"I would rather they'd done something. Ignoring the whole thing was worse."

"I can see the wind blowing. In your painting," Bailey said, reaching out to touch it. "The whole thing is vibrating."

"Congratulations," Sam said with a smile. "You're officially high."

"At least I didn't throw up."

Sam turned to Bailey. "How does it feel, Virgin Mary?" She asked with a smirk.

Before she could stop herself, Bailey lunged in and kissed Sam on the mouth. It happened faster than either of them expected and lasted longer than Bailey had intended. She had never kissed anyone she wasn't related to before that moment, and never on the mouth. Everything was wet, sloppy, and smelled like weed. Although she couldn't say what she expected it to be like, Bailey knew this was not it.

Sam pushed Bailey away.

"The fuck," she said.

Bailey froze, trying to remember to breathe. "I'm sorry," was all she could manage to say.

"Fucking high," Sam muttered as she threw the spray cans back into her bag. She walked back over to Bailey, snatched the joint from her hand and ground it into the broken tile floor.

"I'm done." Sam said.

They walked together but separate, Bailey a few strides behind Sam, heading back towards what they believed was the way out. Whether it was the weed or the rush of kissing her best friend, that lilting feeling had evaporated and she was left with a heaviness, a guilt and her parents' voices echoing endlessly in her head.

She counted her steps, listening to the broken glass crunch beneath her sneakers.

~

Before long, the pair of girls had become lost in the maze of corridors and retail displays. They had entered a section with no skylights or any hint of the outside light to guide their way.

"You sure this is the way out?" Bailey asked, breaking the silence between them.

Sam kept walking, whipping her flashlight across the abandoned space.

Bailey couldn't be sure in the dim light, but there seemed to be more water in this part of the mall. She slipped on something and fell, her knees splashing in the shallow flood water.

Sam turned around, throwing a cone of light over her friend. Her face twisted in disgust.

The flashlight showed the remains of a fish under Bailey's feet, now torn apart and spread up her shoe and pants leg.

"Shoot," Bailey squealed. The smell tore into her nostrils, the smell of decay and death.

Sam scoffed and turned around, walking further into the darkness.

Bailey stomped her leg as hard as she could, trying desperately to get the fish's remains off of her. She shone her light around the space and counted at least five more fish, all dead and rotting around them.

"Watch your step," Sam said as she punted one of the fish carcasses into a display window.

"It's not funny," Bailey said.

"You'll live."

"My parents will ask about where I've been now."

Sam turned around. She stared at Bailey, then, with a running start, punted another dead fish towards her. The fish corpse flew through the air, just inches from Bailey's head. Sam laughed again.

"Goddammit, Sam." She hadn't meant to curse. The word just came pouring out of her mouth. Maybe it was the rising fear or the stress from not understanding why Sam reacted the way she did to their kiss. Whatever the reason, the word felt good rolling across her tongue, like something cold and soothing over a wound.

Sam laughed, more sinister than playful. "So you do curse," she said. "Is that the Third commandment? Don't take the Lord's name in vain?"

"What's your problem?" Bailey asked.

"Fuck it," Sam said, continuing to walk away.

"Do you want me to apologize?"

"It's gonna be too dark to see in here soon."

"Because I am sorry," Bailey said, almost screaming. "I'm sorry you're being such a…" Bailey paused, gathering her strength and will. "Such a cunt," she finished.

"I'm out of here," Sam said. She shouldered her bag and walked away.

Bailey knew she had pushed too hard and was about to lose the only person who knew her more deeply than maybe she knew herself.

"You didn't deserve that," Bailey called out. "You didn't deserve to be ignored."

Sam turned and rushed back towards Bailey, stopping inches from her face. She jabbed her finger into Bailey's sternum. "I know that, God don't I know that," she said, her eyes now shining like glass. "And I'm not your experiment, your lesbian friend you can just test out your feelings on." She walked a few steps, picked up a dead fish, and threw it at Bailey, this time aiming for her head.

Bailey dodged the incoming carcass. She fought back the lump rising in her throat. "What do you want from me?" she called back.

"To fuck off," Sam said.

And, at that, Bailey was alone. Sam turned down a dark corridor and disappeared, leaving Bailey standing, the only thing living in this part of the world. One sharp inhale was all it took for every emotion inside her to come pouring out. She wept for being alone, for being impulsive, for getting high and kissing the only person who she actually liked. Her father had always preached that God knew everything about us, even the ugly parts. But he loved us anyway. Sam had heard Bailey curse, seen her breaking windows, smoking pot, even felt her kiss. She wasn't even sure that God knew her that well, but Sam knew those things had always been deep inside her, buried beneath the layers of piety and spiritual repression.

Finally, there were no more tears to cry, and Bailey looked around her, putting together a plan to get out of this new hell. On her own, the mall seemed darker, more twisted and dingy. Without the bustle of shoppers and the glow of artificial lights, she couldn't place herself or figure out which way to go to leave.

"Didn't even find any wild dogs," she said to herself.

She walked for a few minutes, taking in the collapsed storefronts and broken shelves. She followed the flood line, a perfect horizon etched into the walls, running from one end of her new world to the other. She thought about Noah and his ark and wondered if he had cried at the endless ocean around him. If he woke up every morning and cursed God for choosing him to suffer with the responsibility of saving the world.

The smell nearly knocked her off her feet. Everything in the mall smelled of decay and light touches of death, but here the air was soaked with it. Bailey turned to see a store front, windows intact and doors chained shut. The sign above read "Matt's Pet Store."

A hand touched her and Bailey jumped and screamed.

"Jesus," Sam said.

Bailey caught her breath, her heart still leaping in her chest. "I thought you left," she said.

"I can't leave the Virgin Mary in here by herself."

"I'm fine."

Sam looked at the storefront. "What's in there?"

"Smells like death."

"I can't handle this," Sam said.

Bailey chuckled. "All the stuff you did and this is where you draw the line?"

"Fucking sicko," Sam said. "What do you want to see some dead animals for?"

Bailey didn't answer. She rummaged the cutters out of her backpack and clipped the chain that held the door shut. It fell to the ground, and Bailey swung open the glass doors.

The smell of death rushed to meet the two girls, so rank and powerful that they both gagged in the doorway. After a few seconds, Bailey clicked on her flashlight and stepped into the store while Sam protested behind her, before following suit.

Lining the wall were fish tanks, some empty and some filled to the limit with green and brown floodwater as small, colorful fish floated on the surface, motionless and silent. New algae covered every glass surface and display, creating a green glow throughout the room. The small space had been stacked with crates and cages, no organization or regard for which animals should be separated.

Among the crates and cages were the bodies of the dead. Birds, cats and some dogs lay soaked and bloated in various poses, mouths agape and tongues swollen with decay. Flies buzzed in every direction creating a low humming soundtrack to the room.

"Fucking assholes," Bailey said, surprising herself again, but not finding another set of words to do justice to the scene in front of her.

Behind her came the sound of heaving and vomit splattering. Bailey turned to see Sam doubled over, her face wet and sick and void of any color. She wiped her mouth with her hand. "Who would do this?" she asked.

Bailey covered her mouth with her t-shirt and moved to the back of the store, looking at each enclosure and each dead body. Finally, she came to one cage, tucked into the back of the store, big enough for a small dog. The name plate read "Biscuit" and the door was open, still swinging despite the light rust on the metal.

"Look," Bailey said, excited.

Sam refused to go any further into the pet store. "You got what you need, sicko?"

"He made it out," Bailey said. "Biscuit got out. He survived." Bailey's eyes watered again. She thought about Biscuit, though she didn't know what he might have looked like. With a name like Biscuit, he must be small, she figured. In her mind, she saw him pop open the cage and scamper out as the water rose. He would be a great swimmer, and he would've found a way out.

Sam had sidled up next to her, carrying the smell of sick and sweat with her. Her brown eyes squinted and her mouth curled into a smile.

"Good boy, Biscuit," she said.

~

Both girls walked through the parking lot, the twilight sky darkening above their heads. Bailey knew her parents would be looking for her now. There would be a lengthy lecture waiting for her when she got home. She wondered what Sam's parents would do. Would they reprimand her for staying out so late or would they ignore her as she sauntered into their home.

They stopped on the grassy hill above the mall. Bailey wondered if this were where she and her parents stood in the days after the flood, where she saw Sam's parents weeping and embracing each other. The smell of vomit clung to Sam, just like the smell of dead fish did to Bailey. Neither would dare to look at the other. Instead, they stared at the mall at the bottom of the hill. Bailey traced the flood line that divided those parts of the building that had been destroyed from those parts that hadn't. In the dark it was faint now, barely visible, as if the distinction between what had been flooded and what hadn't didn't really matter. There was no division in reality, no damned and saved. There was only her and Sam and the dog Biscuit, the ones who had escaped.

She smiled. Not because of anything she now knew about herself or her faith. She smiled because she could feel Sam's hand clasped to hers, their fingers intertwined with one another. And that warmth and goodness was, to her, worth any destruction she might face.

The Last Dreamer

The two dirt bikes roared through the open forest, scattering dust, twigs, and smoke across the forest floor, as restless and untethered as the boys who piloted them. Covered by the hardwood canopy, the boys darted between saplings and sunlit patches of wild grass heading deeper into the forest with every twist of their throttles. Despite the noise of the small displacement engines, Jesse could hear the entire forest moving, breathing maybe, the slow steady sound of expansion as the sun started its descent into the dusk hours. A low hum that rose and fell with every bump and banked turn, so palpable, that Jesse soon found himself breathing along with it.

It had been Cotter's idea to cut through the forest. The older boy, now pulling away on his own bike ahead of Jesse, insisted on the forest as a shortcut, a way to enjoy the scenery on the way to their destination. Besides, he'd said. It'd been Cotter who'd found the work in the first place, so he should lead the way.

Jesse eased the throttle on his bike, coming to a stop. The forest had stopped breathing around him, and he found himself waiting for an exhale that would never come.

"Slow up," he called out.

Cotter's bike grumbled to a stop, and the older boy looked back at Jesse. "What's the matter, Cochise?"

"Battery is shifting around on me."

"Cinch it up. We're losing daylight."

Jesse adjusted his own backpack then said, "Who's all this for?"

"Jackson Matte. I told you that."

Jesse adjusted the bungie cords on the used car battery mounted to the back of his dirt bike. They'd spent all day buying supplies for Jackson Matte, perusing through every drug store and grocery store in Moncks Corner with very specific instructions: Cold medicine. Lighter fluid. Nail polish remover. Car batteries and old cookware from the dump. And the boys had found each piece.

"What's he gonna do with all this?" Jesse asked.

"I gotta spell it out for you?" Cotter scoffed.

"I guess not," Jesse said. He finished tying down the car battery. "How often we supposed to make these runs?"

"You want the money or not?"

"I'm just asking is all."

Cotter sighed with all his world-weary wisdom. "You don't ask questions about Jackson Matte," he said. "You do what he needs, then you get paid."

Cotter told Jesse they'd be acting as couriers of sorts, running supplies to a workshop near the edge of Awendaw on the other side of the forest. Though, he'd never mentioned what kind of supplies or for what purpose they were running. "Just simple stuff," he'd told Jesse. "Cold medicine, lighter fluid, glass bottles. Small stuff."

Jesse mounted up on his dirt bike again, trying to push Jackson Matte and all his supplies out of his mind. If there were someone in Berkeley County who didn't know Matte's name, they still knew his workshop. Kids traded stories on the playground about the small spare building on the edge of the lake, the one that smelled like cat piss, the same one that their parents dropped by on their weekly errands. But few knew the man Matte and his penchant for violence. Some of the kids at Jesse and Cotter's school had seen it firsthand in the bloody faces and cracked limbs of their parents.

"Do you hear that?" Cotter called?

"Hear what?"

Cotter shushed his partner and pointed to the sky. Within a few seconds, Jesse could hear the sound too. A low buzzing rattled above their heads, soft at first, then louder until the unmistakable sound of an airplane roared overhead.

The plane, a single engine Cessna, skimmed the top of the pines around them, shearing branches and sending debris raining down on the boys. For a moment, the sky turned ink black as smoke from the plane plumed in all directions. The roar of its engine and the rush of the wind behind it made the boys cover their ears. And just as fast as it cut into their view, it was gone, heading towards wherever its final resting place might be.

Cotter cursed, then screamed at his friend, "Did you see it?"

"How could you not?" Jesse snapped back, his ears still ringing.

"Think anyone's hurt?" Cotter asked?

"Dead, likely."

Cotter looked overhead, clocking the sun's position to the west.

"We got like three hours before dark." He trailed off.

"No way. You said we have to get to Matte's workshop."

"There could be a reward. Like a finder's fee."

"We're gonna get lost."

"You're like part Indian though, right?"

Jesse stared at his friend.

"Be at one with the forest, Cochise," Cotter said.

Somewhere back in his family there was tribal blood. At least that's what his mother had always said. But he never felt at one with the forest the way the Indians in the movies always did. In fact, his mother seemed to avoid the forest as much as she could, sometimes taking unusual routes to avoid crossing through its borders.

The north end of the forest was dense, tightly packed with pine, poplar, and three feet of underbrush. Their bikes were fast enough to beat the dark. But somewhere in his body, Jesse felt a vibration of fear. The forest had a way of turning on you, blocking out the sun or covering up tracks. They were just as likely to ride into a hidden marsh as they were to find that plane. But against his fear, an illogical urge set fire to his fingers and warmed his legs against the forest shade.

Before his brain could form any more rejections, his foot kicked the two-stroke motor to life, sparking the forest with noise. A sharp, quick pain made him wince and check the skin on his leg. There, just beneath the bike, were a few drops of his own blood on the forest floor, drawn from the sharp edges on his dirt bike. Jesse knew it would stop bleeding soon, so he wrung the throttle, breathing the engine to life.

Cotter grinned and started his own bike. The two boys rode north into the forest, off the trails they knew and into the underbrush so as not to leave any noticeable trace of their existence among the late afternoon light.

~

Jesse had recurring nightmares, and so he rarely slept all the way through the night. Most nights, the dreams were standard fare, that feeling of being chased or hunted, and waking right before being caught or consumed by whatever monster lived in his subconscious at the time. But just before his mother died, he began dreaming of a forest, possibly the same one he and Cotter found themselves in now, but he couldn't be sure. Every night he dreamed of the same forest, the trees thick hardwoods and the underbrush wild and untouched. After she died, his dreams became darker, more frantic. His nights were plagued with violence and death, people and animals alike torn apart and consumed by some ancient predator that called the forest home.

The night before he and Cotter saw the plane go down in the Francis Marion Forest, he slipped into one of those dreams where everything feels more real than reality does. He was in the forest, and this time he was running. Though he couldn't see it, he could feel something behind him, haunting each step. So he ran faster. Jesse could feel the scrape of the branches and the forest floor disintegrating under his bare feet. Eventually, the forest opened into a swamp. Small knuckles of cypress roots and saplings bulged from the algae. Out in the middle of the swamp, sat a single engine Cessna, torn apart at the wings and lodged deep into the mud. The pilot had been thrown from the cockpit. The water around the plane moved, rippling and lapping at the shredded fuselage as a thin shadow rose out of the swamp, stretching and cracking into a figure with black eyes and arms as long and spindly as it's body. A comforting scent, sage and cedar, filled his nostrils. Every hair on his body stood at attention as a woman's voice whispered into his ear.

Faster than your dreams.

~

The boys rode in a parallel line, their bikes buzzing happily in the summer air and the occasional sound of glass jars and boxes of cold medicine gently rattling against each other. As they rode through the forest, Jesse could still hear the words in his memory, smell the scent of sage and cedar all around him, the tall hardwoods and unchecked undergrowth, and he became convinced this was the forest from his dreams.

Jesse and Cotter grew up hearing old timers spinning yarns about men and women who wandered into the forest and never came out and of evil spirits and ghosts that had lived in the forest since before people ever set foot in these lands. Jesse's father never taught his son to believe in anything of that sort. In the rare moments that he paid any attention to his son's coming and going, Jesse's father would tell him that the north side of the Francis Marion forest was dangerous. He knew that the forest was dense, with acres upon acres of old pines that disoriented hikers and blocked out the sun, making it impossible to tell which way was north or east or west. He told his son there were no such thing as ghosts or demons or spirits wandering the forest. Instead, his father told him there were places where the underbrush was so thick that you could stumble your way into an ancient swamp and drown with no one around to hear you call for help. He taught his son that the only ones who would ever find your body would be the gators or foxes who called the forest home.

But curiosity is a powerful engine, and doubly so in young boys with enough freedom to go where they are drawn but not enough experience to know when to stop.

Jesse and Cotter slowed to a halt at the edge of a fire road, a long dirt path that stretched forever in either direction.

"Shit," Cotter said. He pointed to the tire tracks, newly printed in the dirt.

"Fire crews?" Jesse asked.

"Or joy riders."

Jesse took his opportunity.

"They look fresh. Probably already there," he said.

Cotter looked down either side of the road.

"Let's pack it in. Matte is gonna be looking for us soon."

"He can wait," Cotter said. "We can't be that far."

Jesse knew that Jackson Matte did not wait for anyone. His reputation for violence was only overshadowed by his impatience. Jesse's imagination ran away from him, elaborating on all the inventive ways Jackson Matte could remind them how much he hates waiting.

"What are you gonna do with a plane, anyway?" Jesse asked.

Cotter smiled at the other boy. "Where's your sense of adventure?"

A light wind flowed down the fire road, obscuring the tire tracks in front of them. It moved steadily, like the forest was breathing, inhaling the boys' scents and discerning their motives. A whisper filtered through the trees and raised the hairs on his neck. There were no words in the whisper, none that he could understand at least.

"Did you say something?" Cotter asked.

"No," Jesse said.

The other boy shrugged and twisted the throttle of his bike.

"Come on," he said, and rode across the dirt path and through the trees on the other side.

Jesse picked up his feet and rode after him. Somewhere in the exhaust fumes of his dirt bike, he could swear there was the scent of sage.

~

Jesse's mom had also been a dreamer. Since she was his age, she would wake up at least two times during the night, sometimes with a loud start and sometimes gently. She never told anyone about the worst dreams, those plagued with scenes of violence and cruelty. Through her adolescence and into adulthood, she learned a valuable lesson: no one has the patience to listen to bad dreams. So she kept those to herself.

She had, unknowingly and unwillingly, passed down her dreams to her son, though he had not yet learned to keep the bad ones to himself. When the nightmares came, more violent and disturbing each time, Jesse cried out for his mother and she would pad quietly across the floor to his room. On the worst nights, his mother would light a small bowl of sage and cedar chips, wafting the smoke in every direction as she prayed prayers that her mother had passed down and her mother and so on, a language so ancient that time had forgotten its meaning. The smell calmed Jesse's mind and set him back on the path to rest.

"You and I, we're not like your dad," she'd told him one night. "We have a gift."

"What kind of gift?" Jesse asked.

She smiled as sweet as honeysuckle. "We can see," she said. "Our people have always been able to see what others can't."

Jesse didn't understand. But he nodded anyway.

"We were the first people in this land, and so we know it better than anyone else. It speaks to us."

"In dreams?"

"Yes."

Jesse rubbed his eyes until they opened fully. "Are they good dreams?"

His mother's head dipped a little, and her bones seemed to grow limp. "Sometimes," she said. His mother picked up the small bowl, still smoking and wafted its essence around his bed.

"What does it do?" Jesse asked, nodding to the smoking bowl.

"My mother used to do this. For protection against the bad dreams." She paused again. "In your dreams, what do you see, Jesse?"

Jesse hesitated. "The woods," he said finally.

"And the shadow?"

Jesse's hands gripped his covers tighter. "Yes."

His mother began to cry, then stroked his hair. "My mother used to tell me that dreams weren't real, that they couldn't actually hurt us." She sniffed. "She used to say that it's in our blood. Something that we carry that goes back a thousand years."

Jesse steadied his breathing, trying to be strong for both of them.

His mom wiped her face with the back of her hand. She set the bowl of sage and cedar next to his bed. "You only need to be faster than your dreams," she said.

She kissed his forehead and Jesse soon fell asleep.

The next morning, he woke to screaming. Jesse ran to the bathroom where he found his father hunched over the bathtub, clutching his mother's naked body. The bloody water sloshed in every direction as his father shouted at Jesse to get help. Jesse's mind evacuated from his body, leaving him standing still, staring at the deep gashes in his mother's arms. It wasn't his father's shouts that brought him back but the smell of sage and cedar wafting up into his nostrils, the smell still drifting through the house from his mother's smudging. His mind rushed back into his body, and all he could do was weep.

~

"My mom used to have dreams about this place."

Jesse grappled with a branch above his head. Cotter stood below him. They had lost the trail about a half mile back and decided to see if they could still spot the rising smoke from the crash. Cotter had suggested that Jesse, who was smaller, should climb one of the ancient pines for a better view.

"She dreamed about the forest?" Cotter asked.

"Nightmares." Jesse ascended as quickly as his adolescent body would let him. He couldn't explain why he was saying this now. Something about the forest quickened his heart and made him more excited. Talking through it seemed like the only way to keep his focus.

"Shit," Cotter said. "You see anything up there? Fire crews can't be that far behind."

Jesse felt the tree sway beneath his weight. He could see just above the pine canopy and through a small clearing just a half mile ahead.

"No fire crews."

"Let's get there first then."

Jesse lowered himself branch by branch. "What do you want to find?" he asked as he reached the ground.

Cotter straddled his dirt bike. "Whatever's there," he said.

Both boys wrung their throttles and sped off toward the plane. The small thumper engines cut through the silence of the forest, sending every creature into a frenzy of fear and delight. The pines began to give way to knobby cypress roots and ground became soft. The knobby tires, well worn by a week of runs to Jackson Matte's workshop, struggled to find grip in the rising mud.

Jesse called out and signaled for Cotter to slow down.

"Swamp up ahead," he said over the bumble of the engines.

Cotter nodded, and the boys slowed to a measly pace, sliding every which way in the loosening soil.

My mom used to have nightmares about this place. His own words echoed in his head. Every tree or hanging moss seemed familiar to Jesse. Not because he'd seen it before, but in the way that a forest can disorient and turn a person around. More than anything else, the smell sent him reeling into his own dreams, into the image of the lanky shadow rising out of the tepid water. Without really knowing, he knew that something was out there.

He whispered to himself, just barely louder than the dirt bike engines. "Dreams are just make-believe."

Be faster than your dreams.

His mother's voice moved through him, echoing in his ears like a dream in stereo. Just louder than a whisper but as clear as if she were right next to him. Jesse whipped his head around, looking side to side. In his panic, his hands twisted the handlebars and the front tire caught a thick patch of mud, sending him high side over the front of the dirt bike.

Cotter skidded in the mud and doubled back.

"What happened?" he asked.

"Hit a mud patch," Jesse lied. He righted the bike and checked his backpack, making sure the contents were untouched.

Cotter helped Jesse pick up his dirt bike. After a moment of silence, he looked to either side of them, as if he were scanning for any authority figure. He unzipped his own backpack and produced a plastic bottle, half-filled with amber whiskey. Jesse knew the brand, the same one his father kept in the high cupboard above their stove at home.

"I wouldn't drink that," Jesse said.

Cotter unscrewed the lid. "Why not? Risked life and limb nicking this from my parents."

"I heard Old Man Hatcher went blind from that stuff."

Cotter considered the warning, then said, "he drank like a fish for forty years. One drink won't make you go blind." He sipped the rim. The drink sent him into a fit of coughing and swearing. Jesse laughed and, never one to be outdone, he grabbed the bottle and sipped.

Every nerve in his body lit up at the same time. The liquid went down hot and burned the whole way down his throat and into stomach. When he exhaled, he felt like a dragon, breathing fire into the air.

"Tastes like gasoline," Jesse said, coughing and trying to catch his breath.

"It might be," Cotter sputtered, his eyes filling with tears, his nose running onto his lip.

Both boys laughed again, coughing between each smile.

Cotter smiled at Jesse, then counted, "One, two, three, go!" Jesse took a long drag from the bottle. Jesse was able to swallow some of it, but the burning sensation overcame him, and he spat the majority into the air and onto the ground. Cotter grabbed the bottle and Jesse counted him down with much the same results. They took a second to recover themselves.

"We can't be far," Cotter said, mounting his bike again.

Jesse motioned to Cotter for the bottle. He took another quick swig, and this time, his eyes still watered, but it went down smoother. He wondered if he had burned off his taste buds. His father used to joke about drunk Indians and, even though he never met his maternal grandfather, Jesse knew his reputation as a heavy drinker. Anytime his mother would mention her father, a wash of sadness came over her face. Jesse put his new fears of alcoholism aside. He started his bike and revved the engine to burn out the excess gas from the carburetor.

Faster than your dreams.

This time, the voice was no longer a whisper but a cascade of sound. Jesse shook, whether from the shock or the whiskey, he didn't know. The bottle fell from his hand, and Cotter rushed over to salvage what was left, fussing about wasting a good time. The same voice that rang as clear as day to Jesse seemed to have passed over Cotter entirely.

"What's got you spooked?" Cotter asked.

Jesse looked around the wetlands, searching the long grass for anything to ease his mind, a strong wind or wild animal calling through the dusk air But there was nothing.

Faster than your dreams.

The voice echoed again. Every insect or trilling animal went silent. The only sound he could hear was the distant buzzing of his own dirt bike. Jesse shook, micro tremors rolling across his skin as he waited for something, anything to make a sound.

A white figure shot across his path, and he screamed and closed his eyes. Jesse counted.

One. Two. Three. Four. Five.

When he opened them, he saw an egret gliding between the trees. The sound of cicadas and birds overhead rushed back into his ears, and he breathed out the tension in his body.

Old Man Hatcher went blind.

He watched the egret come to rest but not on a branch or in the muddy ground. The white bird perched on the edge of a cast iron bathtub, the same tub where his mother took her own life. The tub was filled to the top, but not with water. He couldn't be sure, but whatever it was had stained the inside of the tub a deep red, and it sloshed from side to side like the storms that move across the ocean. Jesse closed his eyes.

One. Two. Three. Four. Five.

He prayed to some unknown god that the whiskey had run its course and that he would find an empty forest again. Jesse opened his eyes.

A woman sat in the tub, submerged, bathing herself in the crimson water. The egret, bigger than any bird he'd ever seen, stood, perched behind her, mounted like a guardian, some kind of protector of the swamp. The woman looked at Jesse, locking him in place with her eyes, two black and ancient shadows etched into her face. She gripped the sides of the tub and hoisted herself out. Her slim framed body stretched to an impossible height, too tall for any woman he'd ever seen, and her arms hung long and gangly at her side. Streaking down each arm, she wore long gashes down that stretched open as she pushed her weight out of the bloody bath.

One. Two. Three. Four. Five.

When he opened his eyes this time, she was walking towards him. The egret perched itself on her shoulders, opening its wings to frame the woman's head like a lily-white crown. Her black hair cascaded down her body, flowing into the forest floor. The woman stepped over leaves, sticks, roots with ease and grace but somehow still stuttering, as if walking in this way were something new. And though her walk and her frame were foreign, he knew her face.

My mom is dead. Dreams aren't real.

She was not his mother. But whatever she was, she wore his mother's face, her smile, her skin, the small wrinkles carved into her forehead from years of worry and bad dreams. The closer the woman came to him, the more her features looked wrong. The face wasn't a face, but a mask, a dead impression of something that was once real. This thing that wore his mother's face had frayed her face at the edges, stretched her out of proportion to fit its oblong head. His mother's eyes had been replaced with two vacant shadows dripping down her chest and stomach. Her arms reached out to him. The bones stretched and cracked, tearing her skin at the elbow until her knuckles reached the forest floor. Her hands dragged the rest of her terrible frame towards Jesse and called out in a language that he couldn't understand, something ancient and terrible.

One. Two. Three. Four. Five.

He opened his eyes, and the woman was gone. The tub was gone. The egret, now perched on a small cypress knob, opened its normal-sized wings, pushing itself into the air. The empty forest was speaking a language he knew again, and Jesse pressed his lips together to keep his body from shaking.

"Jesse!"

Cotter sat on his bike, still next to Jesse but now wobbling a bit more. Jesse guessed he had taken another drag from the whiskey bottle.

"Let's go," he said, impatient and confused.

Jesse kicked his bike to life and glanced toward where the woman had been just moments ago. His dirt bike rumbled beneath him. The smell of the exhaust mixed with the whiskey still on his breath, making a sickly-sweet aroma.

He had only ever dreamed these things before. His mother had said they were dreamers. But his dreams were becoming visions now, intruding into reality. Was this what had happened to his mother before she killed herself in their home?

We're dreamers, not seers, he thought.

They should leave. The thought grew in his mind until it filled every corner of his consciousness. His dreams were crossing over, and for the first time in his life, Jesse considered that they were being followed, maybe even hunted, through the forest. He knew, with a violent certainty, that this place would kill him.

But something urged him on, and he knew it was urging Cotter as well. Though he didn't have a name for it, something exciting and amazing was pulling him in, promising him deliverance or closure, he didn't know for sure. All he knew was that he had to find that plane.

And it couldn't be more than a few hundred yards ahead of them now. They would be there soon at this pace.

He knew it wouldn't be long now.

~

After his mother committed suicide, Jesse's father was prone to disappear for days on end. When the neighbors threatened to call social services, the boy's grandmother took him in for a summer.

"Where's dad?" Jesse had asked.

"Getting cleaned up," his grandmother replied. "He always was useless," she said about her own son. She lit another cigarette. "Take that as a good lesson, boy," she said.

His grandmother, Lois, lived in a trailer park near Lyon's Beach at the edge of Lake Moultrie. Everything there smelled like smoke and lake water. Every trailer looked to be at the end of its life, roof caving in or siding dripping off the sides. The days were filled with silence. His grandmother was a fond believer that children should be neither seen nor heard. And so, Jesse found himself reading every book he could get his hands on in the solitude of his small room. She hadn't even bothered to set up a proper room for him, but instead had him sleep in her sewing room. She reminded him constantly, "I'm giving up a lot taking you in," though Jesse couldn't imagine how much she actually gave up on his account. This was the summer when he met Cotter.

They were the only kids in the park and took a liking to each other. They played games that boys play and got into trouble like boys do. However, they couldn't make too much trouble or take their exploits too far in public at least. Cotter's parents were ministers at the church nearest the trailer park. The church building had once been a strip club but had been converted to a house of worship when Cotter's parents became born again a few years before. They were always nice to Jesse, inviting him for dinner or to go into town for groceries. Jesse often dreamed that they might adopt him as their own. He thought his grandmother might go along with it.

That was also the summer that his dreams started to get worse.

Every dream that summer was the same. He and Cotter were walking through the forest until it gave way to swamp. Cotter disappeared, and he would be left alone, standing in knee deep, still water. The water would slosh as a current of ripples broke around him. When he looked up, a tall shadow was moving towards him, arms out-stretched, calling out to him. He would wake up just as the creature pushed him into the swamp, just before the water filled his lungs.

"What's wrong, Jesse?" Cotter's mom asked one day while they perused the grocery store aisle.

"Yeah, why you such a space cadet?" Cotter asked laughing.

His mother reprimanded her son, then smiled at Jesse.

After a moment, Jesse responded, "Bad dreams."

Cotter's mother nodded. "Sometimes our dreams mean the Lord is trying to talk to us. Would you like to tell me about it?"

Cotter filled the cart with an armful of colorful cereal boxes.

Jesse watched his friend fill up the buggy, imagining family breakfasts and laughing around the table with people who loved him.

"I'm lost in a swamp. Then I see a monster. Then I wake up."

"That sounds very scary," Cotter's mom said, slapping her son's hand as he reached for another box of cereal.

"My mom had dreams too," Jesse finally said.

Cotter's mother fell silent. His mother's suicide was well known in their community. Eventually, he had become used to the silence that followed any mention of her name. Truth be told, he enjoyed the quiet.

After an appropriate amount of silence, Cotter's mother asked, "Were they bad dreams like yours?"

Jesse nodded.

The next day, he went to Cotter's house, expecting to invite his friend to throw bottles into the lake or smash windows in one of the abandoned trailers on Lyon's Beach. Instead, he entered the home and found the living room full of serious-looking adults, all staring at him, all of them wearing those sad smiles that adults wear when they pity a child.

"These are our church friends," Cotter's father said. "Tammy told us about the dreams you and your mom shared. You've gone through a lot. Losing your mother like that, moving in with your grandmother. We all knew and loved your mother. But her dreams and visions…" he trailed off for a moment. "We believe that she was spiritually oppressed, and we love you too much, Jesse, to let those same demons steal your soul." He smiled at Jesse, a genuine, but predatory smile nonetheless. "We'd like to help you, to ask the Holy Spirit to cleanse those demons from your mind."

Jesse wanted nothing more than to dart from the room, but instead, he froze in place. He was surrounded, all eyes glued to him. The feeling was familiar, one that he'd felt many times in his dreams.

Cotter's father took Jesse by the arm, as gentle a touch as Jesse had ever felt, and led him into the circle of serious-looking adults. One by one, each one placed a hand on his head and shoulders, and they explained that they would take turns praying over him. The weight of their hands pressed him to his knees. Their fingers dug into his shoulders. As the first adult prayed, her voice rose and the echo of "amens" voices became more heated and pleading. Every hand gripped him tighter and tighter.

Then they began shouting in a language he had never heard. He wasn't sure if they even knew what they were saying. The words sounded ancient and nonsensical at the same time. One of the adults, a stubby blonde-haired woman caked in makeup, said that the Holy Spirit was working and moving in the room, giving them heavenly tongues with which to reach the throne of God. Their breath was suffocating, their hands sweaty. He felt this new, heavenly language burrowing into his skin, like ticks looking for a blood meal.

"Cleanse this boy," they said.

"Purge the Devil from his soul, oh Jesus."

"Power in the blood, yes, it's in the blood," they shouted.

His body began to shake, not from any spirits, but from panic. He kept his eyes open the entire time, watching Cotter sitting in the corner, his face scrunched into concern for his friend and annoyance at his parents' latest show. When he did close his eyes, he only saw his mother's body draped in that cast iron tub, his father's face twisted in horror. And behind them both, there was the shadow, its bony arms drooped to the floor, breathing out soot and ash over his parents.

Jesse collapsed in the circle. The adults lifted him up, whispering "amen" over and over to each other. Cotter's father helped Jesse up to his feet and smiled.

"Did you feel the spirit move in you, Jesse? He was moving powerfully in our prayers. I believe you have been delivered, son."

Jesse nodded. He would do anything to make this end.

Each adult hugged him as they left, looking very pleased with their efforts. Finally, only Jesse, Cotter, and his parents remained. Cotter's mother gave Jesse a long hug. Her polyester dress scratched at his skin. Despite the prayers and the ordeal he had gone through, he leaned into her embrace, savoring her smell and touch. Soon, they were both crying, but, Jesse suspected, for very different reasons.

"How do you feel, sweetheart?" she asked.

"I feel fine," Jesse said.

"The Lord is with you now."

Jesse forced a smile. After a moment, he said, "Can I ask a favor?"

"Anything."

"Do you have any sage?"

~

Neither Jesse nor Cotter knew how far they had gone. All they knew for sure was that it had been almost an hour and that they had traveled deeper into the forest than ever before. Jesse wondered if anyone had gone this deep into the forest before them, if they were they the first people to step foot in these woods since the ancestors his mother always talked about.

She had always told him the stories about their blood, that they came from a long line of Native shaman, men and women who could see the future, commune with nature, and lead their people with wisdom and dreams of things that were not yet to come.

When his mother had dreams, she took them seriously, leaning on them to make decisions. His father said she was sick, that there was some ailment that ran in her family. Being the rational man he was, he dismissed her dreams as random with no basis or control over reality. And although Jesse didn't know it, his father would sometimes pray to a god he didn't even believe in that the sickness would pass over his son.

Jesse thought about his father as he wrung the throttle of his dirt bike, moving as fast as the forest would let him. He thought about his father's disappearance, and reappearance, the court hearings, the moving from house to house. Jesse knew his father was trying to outrun the memories, and he hoped that one day he would be able to find peace.

The boys weaved and darted around saplings of oak and pine and poplar, flattening the underbrush in their path. Their engines were the only sound to be heard for miles in any direction. Finally, Cotter, who was leading, stopped.

"I don't think we need to go any further," he said over the idling bike.

In his mind, Jesse agreed. And he had every intention of speaking this agreement. But when he opened his mouth, he surprised himself, saying "We're not that far. Just a bit further."

Cotter threw him a concerned look. Even Jesse found himself confused by his own words. He knew the forest was dangerous, but he couldn't stop now. Though he still couldn't say why.

"Why do you want to find this plane all of a sudden?" Cotter asked.

"Don't be such a pussy." The words came out more belligerent than he'd meant, angry even. He wanted to apologize, but how could he? This was something that Cotter couldn't know or understand. He had to find that plane.

Cotter began to offer another retort, but he stopped and pointed to something behind Jesse.

Inside a small clearing, tucked against a crooked oak, the boys saw a cabin, rotten and collapsing from every angle. Too small to be a ranger's cabin, the cabin looked to be one room, enough for a few people to sit or at least two full-size whiskey stills.

"Old shiner's cabin?" Cotter asked.

Jesse ignored him, laid down his bike, and made his way to the cabin. Cotter began yelling behind him, telling Jesse to stop, to leave it alone. But his voice was as faint as a childhood memory. Jesse walked up to the cabin and ran his hands along the old, decrepit wooden structure. He was surprised to find it wet to the touch. It hadn't rained in weeks. Every tree they passed and every blade of grass crumpled from drought. But this place, the wood paneled along its outside, felt as if it had just come through a long summer storm. Rot was nowhere to be found, only small spots of algae growing amongst the damp wood.

Cotter jogged up beside him. "What the hell is this place?"

Jesse heard his friend's question, but it wasn't important. Now that he had found this place, nothing else was important.

All along the walls were carvings, some new, and some very old. They weren't pictures or any kind of language that Jesse recognized. The symbols carved into the wood were, every one of them, deep and done with great care. Some were stacked together in columns from the roof of the structure to the foundation. Others were small, almost hidden among the larger glyphs. He admired their sharp edges and the places where they flowed and swirled. Although he didn't recognize them, he knew they were exactly what he was looking for. He dragged his hand along a row of large carvings, arching in a complete circle, dug deep into the wet outside of the cabin. Each one buzzed with life, shaking and warming his skin.

"We have to go in," he said.

"I thought we were looking for the plane," Cotter said.

"This is important," Jesse snapped, again louder and more aggressive than he'd meant to.

"I don't like these symbols," Cotter said. Maybe it was because of his religious background or just a keen intuition, but Jesse knew he should trust Cotter in this, but this place entranced him. It was a compulsion that pulled at every cell in his body, begging him to open the door and come inside.

"You hear me?"

Before Cotter had finished speaking, Jesse had opened the door.

Are you faster than your dreams?

The inside was wonderful and familiar. A thick carpet stretched from corner to corner, and the room was positioned with comfortable furniture and lamps and tables. A family lived in this room, people who loved each other and valued spending time together. There was love and warmth in this room, and it called out to Jesse, tempting him with the one thing he really wanted: a place to belong.

Cleanse those demons from your mind...

It took a moment for him to recognize that this was Cotter's living room. All around him, chants rose through the floor and out of the walls, a language he couldn't recognize, as if a hundred people were praying, pleading. Though he couldn't understand what they were saying, he knew the voices wanted him to step in, to sit on the couch, to relax and let go and be loved and appreciated. He touched the fabric, felt its tweed roughness and smelled the dust lingering in the air. The lamps glowed warm and pleasant in every corner, and the carpet cradled his muddy shoes as he made his way around the furniture, feeling the warmth and buzz electrifying his fingertips.

Every light flickered, subtly at first and then more and more. The door to the living room opened in front him. Jesse threw himself behind the couch, making his body as small as possible. The mud on his hands and shirt marred the clean fabric of the couch and stained the carpet. He hoped that no one would be mad at him. He was afraid, and it was an accident after all.

Heavy footsteps thudded one after another, echoing through the room. Peering above the couch, Jesse saw the top of a man's head, crowned with a slick pompadour hair style, moving around the room. He bobbed like a bird, bouncing up and down and circling as if he were searching the room or following a scent. The man moved with grace but still stuttered with every step, as though walking upright was not a part of his natural process. Though he couldn't see the man's face, and despite his erratic movements, Jesse knew he was a good man, someone with the best intentions and an answer to Jesse's many, many questions.

Cleanse those demons from your mind...

He whispered like the wind.

Jesse was crying now, though he didn't know why. If it was fear, why was he afraid? This was not a place for fear, but for love and deliverance. This man was here to help. Jesse became convinced that this man was the answer. He was here to explain why his nightmares were crossing over into reality. He wanted Jesse to know that there was a path to healing. Jesse knew, that this man was not just a messenger or a prophet, but the Lord himself, the Divine made flesh. And he could bring Jesse to salvation, the same salvation he brought to Jesse's mother.

It's in the blood...

The whispers, the chants, the prayers, they swelled around him like a chorus, no longer dissident, but beautiful, a choir filled with grace and truth and the spirit of love. They called Jesse to raise up and meet his salvation. The Lord has come to save your soul, young man. You only need to accept his free gift of deliverance.

Jesse stood to his feet, ready and willing for his Savior to sweep him up in his arms. And there was his salvation. The man, the Lord himself, stood and glowed, filling the living room with light and warmth and that keen sense of belonging.

It's in his blood...

The man's face was stretched, like his mother's in the woods, pulled taut to fit a larger figure. Where his eyes should be were just shadows, dripping darkness onto the floor and puddling at his feet. But Jesse knew this man. He was kind and loving. He wanted to help. The man reached out his gangly hand, long, slim, and gnarled like old cypress, and Jesse wanted to know him, to listen to his wisdom and hear his stories about the forest and its mysteries. Jesse reached out his own hand, feeling that warmth and comfort pooling up in his fingers.

A boy screaming, hands grabbing him and shaking with ferocity and desperation. Cotter's living room disappeared, and Jesse found himself standing in the middle of the cabin and Cotter staring, his eyes wide and crazed. He looked down. All around him, circling his feet were symbols, carved deep into the wood and colored with white in a perfect circle. The lush carpet, comfortable furniture and soft lighting were gone, replaced with the inside of the damp cabin, dark and mildewed to the edge of its lifespan.

The pain came next, electric and white hot, crumpling Jesse down to his knees. As he grasped his hand to his chest, blood spread across his shirt, soaking through to his skin. He screamed, slow and silent at first then loud and frantic. The forest sounds came rushing back to him, every bird, insect, lizard, and unseen predator seemed to call out with him, spreading his pain through everything that drew breath for miles.

"What the fuck were you doing?" Cotter took off his outer shirt and wrapped Jesse's bleeding hand.

Jesse stuttered, "I don't know." He collapsed onto the cabin floor. Something fell from his hand, clattering amongst the buzzing symbols all around them.

"Looked like you were trying to cut your hand off," Cotter said.

"What?"

"You grabbed a piece of wood and pushed it into your hand. Like you were trying to crucify yourself." He finished wrapping his friend's hand and tied off the fabric, tighter than Jesse would've liked.

Jesse's eyes adjusted to the unnatural darkness, and he saw the inside of the cabin for what it actually was. There was no carpet or sofa, no lamps or cozy tables. There was nothing. The one-room cabin was small, spare, and dark. Light peeked through the cracks in the boards, and the windows, long boarded up, leaking with the afternoon light and summer humidity. All along the floors were long smears, earthy brown ribbons of mud and shit. But along the length of the walls, heavy and thick, deep red streaks encircled them now, old blood, dancing high and low but spread with intention and purpose. *Animal blood, a hunting cabin,* he thought. Though his mind wandered with other possibilities. Jesse couldn't imagine that much blood could be inside any one living thing, even something the size of a person.

The same symbols that were carved into the outside had been carved into the inside walls as well. Only here, there were more of them. Many more. It seemed that every inch of wood was covered in the symbols. Some he knew as doodles, simple drawings or initials. Others were, by their design, more sinister, colored in white or red paint, possibly blood. As his head cleared, Jesse could feel what Cotter felt before they'd entered the door: This place was wrong.

"There's so much blood," he murmured.

"What is happening to you?" Cotter asked.

"I don't know." Jesse fought to keep the tears out of his eyes.

"This place is evil."

Jesse breathed in the moldy air. "It's not the cabin," he said.

"I think it's your head," Cotter said. He sat down next to his friend. "You kept muttering."

"It's in the blood," Jesse whispered. He reached down and picked up the piece of wood he had dropped earlier. It was no bigger than a pencil, but sharp at the point. His blood still dotted the damp wood at his feet, some of it now lining the indentions of the strange symbols.

"We gotta get out of here. Forget that plane." Cotter said.

In his clear state of mind, Jesse said, "No."

Cotter wrinkled his face in confusion, maybe disgust as well.

"I'm not running," Jesse said, tossing the wooden piece at the nearest wall.

"Level with me," Cotter said. In a low whisper, he asked, "Are you seeing things?"

"It's supposed to just be dreams," Jesse said. "It's always been dreams. But now, I can see them when I'm awake."

"Jesse," Cotter said. The sound of his name coming from his friend's mouth was enough to catch his attention. They so rarely used each other's names, preferring, as many young boys do, to defer any seriousness with nicknames or insults. Jesse could see, for the first time, that Cotter was unnerved, shaken by what he'd seen. Something like concern or care softened his face for a moment.

"You ain't well," Cotter continued. "Let's turn back and call it a day. Fire crews probably already got to the plane by now. If we show up with bags full of cold medicine and lighter fluid, they're gonna ask a lot of questions."

Jesse thought about his mother. She'd never said anything about visions, only ever dreams. He wondered if other ancestors had wandered into the forest and lost their way as well as their minds. If the dreams were enough to drive his mother to suicide, what would the visions do to him?

The boys left the cabin, walking out to their dirt bikes, Jesse still clutching his injured hand. Maybe Cotter was right, he thought. Leaving was the sensible thing to do. Even in his adolescence, Jesse had enough of his father's rational mind to know that was true. If his mother were here, she would tell him to leave the forest, go home and never dare to dream again. But she was gone now, and Jesse was alone, the last dreamer left to wander through his life without the wisdom his mother claimed they possessed.

As he mounted his dirt bike, all the talk, the rumors, about his mother ran through his mind. *She was touched. That bad blood got to her.* And he had believed some of them. But the more he dreamed, the less he could explain away his mother's words. And now, plagued with visions and some unknown terror, he felt more lost than ever. He wasn't even sure that his mother would know what to do.

"I have to do this," he said.

"What?"

"Everyone would tell me to leave it alone. But if I do, it'll never stop, and I'll never know."

"Never know what?" Cotter's face drooped to one side.

"I'll never know why us, why me and my mom."

Behind him, Cotter let out a loud and defiant grunt. Then he said, "You obviously can't be trusted to go alone." He reached into his backpack and produced the plastic whiskey bottle. Cotter took a long drag and offered it to Jesse. "For the road," he said.

Jesse hid his smile from his friend and took two long swallows. It burned, but in warm comforting way this time. The boys mounted their dirt bikes and cinched up their backpacks. Cotter tried his kick starter. But instead of starting, the little two stroke sputtered and stalled. He thrust his entire body weight into lever. The engine groaned then died. He sniffed the cylinder head and ran his finger along the seal.

"Oil leak," he said. "Try yours."

Jesse tried the kick starter on his own bike to the same results. A small trickle of dark fluid dripped from the bottom of the engine.

Cotter cursed.

"Let's go," Jesse said, pushing his bike past his friend. His heart was still racing, and the man's face, stretched and contorted and hiding the creature's own face flashed in his mind with every step. All he could think about was that feeling of salvation, the warmest and most comforting feeling he'd ever felt, something like the feeling of coming home after a long trip. The boys had walked thirty yards from the cabin when it occurred to Jesse that his blood was still back there, somewhere, spread across the old cabin floor. And like that cabin, ancient and bound to the evil of the land, his blood would always be part of this forest.

~

After his mother's death, an army of counselors and psychiatrists all lined up to help Jesse through this difficult time. Their assessments were all the same. Give him time, and he'll open up.

Once his father cleaned up, Jesse left Lyon's Beach and moved back home. His grandmother seemed glad to have her sewing room back and left him to wait for his father on the front porch alone. But Cotter and his family were there, keeping him company and offering to help him load his things in the car. They even said a quick prayer for him and his father, though the boys exchanged knowing glances and chuckled through the whole thing.

It didn't take Jesse long to forget his mother's advice and her remedies. They hadn't helped her, so why would they help him? His father, a rational man steeped in depression and guilt, had no time for Jesse's questions, and Jesse knew better than to ask. His father was not a violent man, and there was no meanness in him. There was, since his wife had taken her own life, nothing in him. Jesse had found him many nights sitting up in his chair, watching the static on the television, as if he were trying to discern signs and messages in the noise.

It would be weeks before the dreams would start back again though. Maybe because he was wrapped in the busyness that follows death, but he didn't seem to have the time or energy for dreams. But within a few weeks, when his father was well-situated in neglect and silence, Jesse began to dream again.

At first, they were vague and undefined. But each night, they became more contoured and detailed. There was the forest. In the forest was the swamp. But the swamp rippled with movement. Something he couldn't see or explain parted the water and rustled the branches every night, crossing endlessly from one end to the other. Occasionally there were others, animals that wandered in and disappeared just as quickly.

One night, when the dreams had taken full shape and definition, Jesse saw a man, lost and wandering among the trees. The man had no face or any striking features, but Jesse could see the glint of moonlight off the nickel plated pistol in the man's hand. Somehow, Jesse could feel the evil that radiated from the man's mind and the black intentions that seeped his heart. Jesse hated this man though he didn't know him. He knew this was a bad man and that he was doomed.

The creature gave chase to the evil man, moving as swift and quiet as a shadow. The same black limbs and knobby fingers traced their way through the black water, brushing aside the lilies and moss that floated along the surface.

Faster than your dreams…

The creature repeated this over and over as it stalked the man, adorning it's body with faces, all stretched and pulled taut against its frame. The creature changed faces the way a person changes their shoes or puts on a smile, and each one frightened the man more than the last until he began to sprint through the shallow water, ducking and dodging branches and roots jutting out in every direction.

The man lost his breath after only a few minutes of running. The swamp went quiet and the man wondered if he was safe. He doubled over, breathing hard and heavy when another figure stepped out from the underbrush. The man called him Scott. He seemed relieved and glad to see Scott and the two men embraced. To the man's horror, Scott's arms stretched and cracked, splitting the skin at his joints. His eyes became shadows as dark and deep as the swamp itself. The face he wore stretched and swirled around the creature's own head. The man screamed as the creature grabbed him and pushed him into the deep mud of the swamp. His body merged with the muck and the swamp until there was no man, only the memory of one. And when he was gone, the creature swallowed Scott's face, disappearing again into the nighttime shadows.

When he woke up, Jesse emptied their spice cabinet, digging until he found a small container of sage. He used twine and bound the sage leaves together. With his father's lighter, he burned the leaves and waved them in every direction in his room, spreading the ashes along his bedspread. When that was done, he laid down again, his heart beating fast and heavy. When he eventually went back to sleep, he didn't dream of anything, no creatures or swamps, only the sweet emptiness of a deep sleep.

Whenever he thought of that dream, Jesse felt a rumbling of something awful creep up his spine. The violence and horror of it stuck with him as it would any boy of his age. However, as he reminisced on that dream, he began to understand what it was that really terrified him: that whatever the creature was, with it's knobby fingers and whispering voice, could feel him there too. That maybe it was waiting for him to return, not in dreams, but to the forest itself.

~

The sun had begun to set behind the trees, giving the forest a golden glow from edge to edge. But in a forest this old and this tall, the dark would creep up long before the sun set below the horizon. So as Jesse and Cotter pushed their bikes between the trees and undergrowth, they were losing light with every step.

"Tell me what happened," Cotter finally said, breaking a silence that had carried for at least ten minutes.

Jesse didn't answer.

"Tell me," Cotter repeated.

Even if he'd wanted to tell Cotter, he wouldn't know where to begin, how to describe the creature and its hands, the faces it wore and how it wriggled its way into his memories to turn them against him.

Cotter stopped and threw his dirt bike to the ground. "I know we ain't like, best buddies, but if I'm gonna be out here with you, I need to know if you're gonna off yourself or something."

Jesse kept walking.

"You going crazy?"

"I might be," he whispered. The more he thought about what he'd seen, the possibility of him losing his mind seemed more and more likely. After all, isn't that what had happened to his mother? If he truly was as much like her as she seemed to think, it would only be a matter of time before whatever afflicted her caught up with him.

"Why'd you cut yourself like that?" Cotter asked. Something in his voice had shifted. What had sounded like an accusation now seemed more like, at least to Jesse, uncertainty

Jesse breathed in the humid air. "My mom killed herself."

"Yeah. I remember."

"She had dreams. About this place. She used to tell me, 'don't ever go near the forest.' Said there was something in our blood."

"Y'all got some kind of Indian curse or something?"

"Nightmares." He paused a long while, then continued. "Sometimes it's memories, real things that happened. It's supposed to just be dreams. But now it's like it's real, like visions. There's a…" he paused again, judging the depth of their friendship. "A creature."

Cotter stared at his friend and then spit into the dirt. "A 'creature?'"

"Haven't you heard anything weird? Like whispers or like someone talking to you?"

Cotter hung his head. "We need to get out of here." With that said, he picked up his bike and walked past Jesse, leaving him behind.

Jesse followed his friend for a few yards before speaking up again.

"I found her body," he shouted.

Cotter stopped and faced his friend.

"When my mom killed herself, I walked into the bathroom and found her body in the tub. She cut her wrists. There was blood everywhere. My mom's blood on the floor and the rug and on my dad's hands and clothes and every towel we owned." He wanted to fight the tears, but there didn't seem to be a point to it anymore. So he sobbed. "I lost my dad too. He changed. Wouldn't look at me. And everyone pitied me and kept asking 'why'd she do it, why'd she do it.' Like if we knew the reason it would make sense and that would make things better. But it's bullshit. It doesn't change anything." Jesse wiped the tears from his face. "But you were different. You didn't care 'why she did it' and you never brought her up. And it was nice. Because I don't want to think about that ever again. In fact, I'd rather forget she ever lived. 'Cause then I don't have to think about how she died."

For a while, the only sound between them was the animals at dusk, some settling in and others just waking up, filling the silence between the two boys. Though neither of them could put the feeling to words, they knew they were now tethered to each other by the weight of their emotions, the loss of innocence and the breadth of knowledge that comes with grief.

Finally, Cotter spoke.

"That sucks," he said. "About your mom and you."

"Yeah it does," Jesse said. He wiped his nose again with his bandaged hand.

"I don't think you're really crazy," Cotter said. "But a creature…you got to hear it, right?"

Jesse chuckled. "I know," he said.

They both smiled and walked their motorbikes side-by-side through the forest, the contents of their backpacks jangling and ringing through the trees.

Carried on the wind was a familiar scent, and it caught Jesse's attention. It was the smell of sage, his mother's scent and the scent of dreamless sleeps. He propped his dirt bike against a tree and followed the scent to a small clearing. There, bathed in sunset light, was a patch of sage, fresh and green. Jesse picked a handful and stuffed half the leaves into his pocket.

He caught up to Cotter, gripping a handful of the sage leaves.

"Do me a favor," he said, putting the leaves into his friend's hand. "Keep these with you."

"What's it for?"

"You burn it and wave the smoke. If things get weird."

Cotter's face drooped, whether from concern or exhaustion, Jesse couldn't tell. For all of his dad's rational coaching, Jesse held a small place in his mind for his mother's beliefs and all things spiritual. He wanted to believe that she was right in some things, that there was something more to the world around them than just what they could see and hear and touch. Jesse believed she was in this small patch of sage. For all of the darkness and uncertainty of the forest, his mother grew here too. She was the smell of sage surrounding both of them, protecting and sheltering them from whatever might be waiting among the trees.

~

"There are things older than our people that live out there."

Jesse's mother told him stories like this, not every night, but when she was feeling especially nostalgic or anxious. Jesse couldn't understand it at the time, but his mother was haunted, like most indigenous peoples, by the fear of forgetting their cultures and their stories. And so she fought against forgetting by passing those stories on to her son. And like many indigenous peoples, she didn't shy away from the unpleasantness that followed her.

"My grandmother told me stories," she said, "Tales of an evil that haunts our blood living out among the swamps and has for generations."

Jesse listened to his mother, wishing she would stop telling him these things, but also longing for the story to continue.

"Are we Cherokee or Catawba?" Jesse asked. "One of the boys from school says his great grandmother was a Cherokee princess."

His mother laughed. "That's how you know he's white," she said. Then she continued, "Our people were special, a group of healers and seers that other tribes relied on."

"What did they see?"

"Everything that the others couldn't. And your grandmother taught me to see, and I will teach you one day when you're older."

His father's voice boomed from the other end of their small house. "Stop filling that boy's head with that Indian horseshit," he said.

She leaned in closer to her son. She breathed in all his ready-for-bed scents of soaps and toothpaste. "Your father can't understand because he only believes in what his eyes can see. You and I, we are people of the spirit."

Young Jesse considered his mother's words, then asked, "What if what we see are bad things? Scary things?"

His mother kissed him on the forehead and smiled. Though she couldn't tell him, there was an unnatural wisdom in his question. Children with wisdom beyond their years could survive most anything. "You cannot choose what to see. If you could only see the good things in this world, how would you know what is truly good and what is truly evil?"

Jesse, in his child's mind, couldn't grasp the realities of what his mother had told him. But her words washed over him like warm water, comforting, but gone as quickly as they'd come. But he did understand his own wants and feelings then. He understood that he didn't want to see things like his mother or her mother or like the old seers in their history. He wanted to lie in his bed and hear his mother's voice and smell the boozy scents of his father as he drifted to sleep.

But rarely is anyone able to choose their gifts or to what lineage they belong. For Jesse, as he grew older, as he endured his mother's suicide and his father's descent into drugs and self-destruction, he would remember his mother's words differently. For Jesse, those words didn't contain the hope that, perhaps, his mother wanted them to have. Seeing the good things didn't make him appreciate them any more. In fact, seeing the good around him filled him with more anxiety. Because, for Jesse, whenever he experienced the good things in life, it meant the evil things were waiting in line, sharpening their teeth and calling out for his dreams.

~

The sun was minutes away from settling in behind the trees and the boys meandered amongst the forest, hoping and praying to find some landmark or fire road to bring them home. But as they walked further, each step felt to Jesse like it would carry him deeper into the dirt, closer to the evil things waiting for him in the gathering darkness.

Cotter caught the smell first and stopped pushing his bike for a moment.

"Smells like shit," he said.

Jesse stopped and smelled the air. "There's a swamp nearby."

"It's not the swamp."

Jesse's throat tightened and the sweat beaded up on the back of his neck. He thought about his dreams and the man who was dragged into the waters.

"I can't be around the swamp," he said.

"Mess with your chakra?" Cotter said.

Before today, Jesse would've shrugged off the comment or changed the subject. But he and Cotter were irrevocably connected now. While the older boy seemed emotionally stunted, he was the closest thing Jesse had to a friend.

"There's something in the swamp," he said, keeping his voice low.

"Alligators, foxes, crackheads, all kinds of things live in the swamp," Cotter said, laughing to himself.

"There's *something* in the swamp," Jesse repeated.

Cotter's face went hard and straight. "Okay," he said, and they walked a little further until finally, Cotter said, "You think Jackson Matte is out looking for us by now?"

Jesse smirked. "Looking for his supplies, more like." Somehow, the thought of a notorious meth dealer like Jackson Matte made Jesse smile. Maybe, he thought, dealing with a real-life criminal was better than whatever was stalking them through the forest.

Cotter checked the contents of his backpack. "We'll tell him we ran into the law and had to duck out or something. He likes me, so we should be good." He tried the kick starter on his dirt bike for good measure. The bike sputtered then died, leaking the same dark fluid.

Jesse stared at the fluid. Something about the way it caught the light made him pay more attention this time. "I don't think that's oil," he said. The thought had occurred to him when he first saw the bikes leaking back at the cabin. But given the weight of his ordeal, he hadn't thought to mention it.

Jesse tried kicking his own bike to life with the same result, a sputtering engine and the same fluid seeping out of the crankcase. This time, he ran his finger along the seal. The liquid was thin, too thin to be engine oil. He rubbed it between his fingers and smelled.

"It's not oil," he said. But he couldn't bring himself to say, out loud, what it was. More than Jackson Matte or his mother's bedtime stories, he was afraid of what he knew now.

"What is it?" Cotter asked.

Jesse pushed the words out of his mouth. "It's swamp water," he said low and quiet.

Cotter stared at his friend. "We haven't been near the swamp," he said, also keeping his volume down.

Jesse's heart leapt throughout his entire body and his mother's words rang through his head.

Evil that haunts our blood living out among the swamps.

"What the fuck is happening?" Cotter said, looking into the trees above them. But Jesse knew that anything that they should be afraid of, would not come from above, but below, out of the tannin-soaked waters of the swamps and wetlands dotted across the forest.

Cotter sniffed again. "There's that smell again"

"Gasoline," Jesse finished.

Silence held between the boys for a moment. Then Cotter asked, "Do you think it's the plane?"

Just ahead of them, the trees tightened their ranks, pulling close like soldiers guarding the land from view. The underbrush prevented any light from getting through, but the smell persisted. Gasoline mixed with the decay that only an ancient swamp can create. The smell seeped through the branches, and it seemed to pull at Jesse, willing him to cross into its borders. He knew these tricks now, not that it made them any less powerful, but his rational mind knew to hold fast. But then came the voices again.

Faster than your dreams.

"Can you hear it?" Jesse asked?

"I hear the wind," Cotter responded.

"It's in the wind, the voices."

Cotter strained his head, and Jesse could tell he wanted to hear it, to vindicate his friend's claims. But he could tell that Cotter couldn't hear the same voices. Because they came again, a chorus flowing in perfect harmony.

It's in the blood.

Jesse's skin rippled, sending his body into a violent shiver. But he steeled his muscles and his will. After a moment he said, "I'm sick of it."

"What?" Cotter asked.

"Sick of it," his voice shuddered. "Fuck it all," he said.

Cotter stared ahead, breathing his words carefully, unsure of what was really happening. Even in his uncertainty, he joined in. "Yeah," he said. "Fuck it all."

Jesse threw his dirt bike to the ground and tossed his backpack with it. "You hear me?" he screamed. "Ghost, spirit, whatever the fuck you are? Fuck it all and fuck you!"

"Yeah," Cotter said. "Fuck you, swamp!"

After a moment, the woods seemed to hold their breath. Every creature that sang a moment ago went silent, waiting for the exhale. In that brief pause, Jesse thought it might be over. In school they were taught that all it took to handle a bully was to stand their ground, to plant their feet and refuse to be pushed around. Though he hadn't seen it work in school, he thought, for a moment, that maybe it had worked now. Maybe it was his mother's stories or some indigenous blood memory, but he knew he was wrong, that an ancient and unknowable evil was not a school bully.

But silence reigned, continuing for what felt like an eternity to the boys. When they thought it was over, somewhere from deep into the forest, the boys heard another voice.

"*Ayudame.*"

The voice was soft and harsh, like a man who hadn't spoken in days. But it carried as clear and clean as though whoever spoke were standing right in front of them.

Jesse held his breath and, though he didn't regret anything he said, he now regretted being so loud.

The voice came again.

"*Ayudame, por favor.*"

"Is it Spanish?" Jesse asked.

"Yeah," Cotter said.

"What's that mean?"

Cotter's breath came heavy from between his lips. He said, "It means 'help me.'"

~

There were other dreams, ones that Jesse didn't tell anyone about. These were the bad ones, the dreams that stuck with him for days on end. They were violent and old. Men and women being stalked, hunted, and murdered in the swamp as the creature changed its face and stretched out to end their lives. Nearly every night, he woke trying to muffle his screams, filled with panic. He remembered every detail, the sound of their footfalls in the soft earth, every tree and every inch of swamp. After his mother died, he told himself the stories she had told him, always assuring himself that these were just dreams.

But there was now nothing to calm his mind. Now his dreams were real and he had the bloody hand to prove it. Whatever stalked his nightmares was just beyond the underbrush where he and Cotter found themselves.

Even so close to the swamp, the woods twisted and warped the boys' perception to the point where the only thing that was certain was the smell of it; that old decrepit smell of dead things come to rest drew them toward the water.

"Maybe it's the plane pilot," Cotter said, trying to find some hope in the words. He and Jesse were huddled at the edge of the swamp, trying to remain unseen behind a line of ferns.

"We have to leave," Jesse said.

"What if someone's hurt?" Cotter said. "He wouldn't be calling out if he didn't need help."

"*Ayudame, por favor*," the voice called again.

"Let's go," Jesse said.

"What happened to 'fuck it all?'"

Jesse grabbed his friend and held his shirt collar tight between his hands. "These are its hunting grounds," he said quietly, "the place from my dreams."

"You've lost it, Cochise," Cotter said. "Someone is hurt and needs help." He got up and cut through the overgrowth into the shallow end of the swamp.

Although he knew better, by way of advice and intuition, and although his dreams had warned him against these grounds, Jesse couldn't let his friend face what he knew was waiting for them on his own. If they were tethered together, Cotter's fate would be the same as his own.

Jesse followed after Cotter, stepping through the brush, following the decaying scent of the swamp. The boys sunk to their ankles in loose mud and brown water. The deafening sound of insects, reptiles, and amphibians drowned out their own footsteps and heavy breathing. The sun had set overhead, but the swamp was timeless. No light filtered down through the thick cypress branches and the moss that dangled fifteen feet above their heads. This was, Jesse knew, one of the few spots where people had left no mark. Jesse wondered if this was what the world had once been like, before people had staked their claims to the land, back when they let their dreams guide their decisions.

"*Ayudame, por favor.*" The voice called out again, floating in the high humid air. Each syllable croaked with more labor than the last. The voice was clearer though, rising above the resonant wildlife calls.

"Son of a bitch," Cotter said, pointing to a spot just ahead of them.

Sitting in the shallows, wrapped around the trunk of a thick cypress tree was a single-engine plane, the same plane from Jesse's dreams: a single engine Cessna twisted and gnarled from a hard crash into the forest.

Cotter leapt forward, but Jesse caught him by the shoulder. "Wait," he said.

Something about the plane wasn't right. Jesse, in all his teenage wisdom, couldn't exactly pinpoint what seemed so wrong though. Aside from the generations of wisdom that called him to leave that place, his rational side, his father's voice, told him to observe what he saw. And then, saw it.

"How long has this plane been here?"

Cotter seemed confused by the question. "We saw it go down like an hour ago."

Jesse shook his head. "But how long has *this* plane been here?"

Aside from typical crash damage, a bent propellor, twisted appendages, and shattered glass, the plane was overgrown with ivy, moss, and vines. From their vantage point, Jesse could see blooms sprouting from the floor and engine compartment. Any metal not covered in growth was rusted, almost completely through.

"What is going on?" Cotter asked.

"Look," Jesse said, pointing to the side of the plane.

The fuselage had been peeled back, the way his grandma would peel cans of meat for his dinner. And smeared across the side, long dark red streaks reaching all the way to the tail. The old blood in front of them now pulled Jesse's memory back to the cabin. The markings were the same width and length. Whatever had streaked the blood through the cabin had done it here as well.

"Nobody has been in that plane for a long time," Jesse said. The realization fell onto him, breaking his confidence and any sense of reality that he'd once held.

"It was a trick," he whispered. "The plane, the whole thing wasn't real."

"*Ayudame, por favor.*"

Cotter jumped at the voice this time. The once shrill chorus of swamp life had died to a whisper at the sound of the voice. Jesse felt exposed by the silence, as if it had somehow covered their tracks and their presence. He felt unwelcome here.

"You were right," Cotter said. "We have to leave, right now."

Jesse stood up to turn and leave.

Bright fluorescent lights blinded him. He sat opposite a standard issue school desk, wondering how long this would take. The office was cramped. Even though there were only two people in it, Jesse was so cramped he found it hard to take normal breaths.

"Let's talk about your mom," the guidance counselor said.

"I'd rather not," Jesse said.

The voice was one he knew. It was kind and understanding, just the way he remembered. But her face was wrong, although he couldn't understand why.

"Why do you think she took her own life?"

"This isn't right," Jesse said.

"You have to talk these things through if you want to heal," the voice said. He stared at her face until he could see through it. Her features were stretched too thin and warped out of proportion.

"Do you think she was weak-minded? Not fit for the world, perhaps?" she asked.

"Shut up."

"Shut up," the voice echoed. It was no longer the kind voice he remembered, but something deeper and more sinister. The face recollected itself then smiled at him.

"I'm here to help you," she said.

"Everyone says I'm crazy," Jesse said.

"Do you think they could be right?" she said. "In my professional opinion, I think you might be truly crazy."

Jesse found his breath and his nerve. Then he said, "If you're real, then I can't be crazy."

"Shut up," the voice boomed.

The guidance counselor smoothed her hair, gleaming like plastic in the bright lights. "Do you think your mother would've killed herself if she loved you?"

Jesse fought the tears welling behind his eyes.

"It's okay to cry," the guidance counselor said.

"You killed her. You took her from me," Jesse finally said.

"You killed her," the voice echoed. "You took her."

"She was a dreamer, and you took her from me."

Seer. It's in the blood.

His hands were wet and water dripped down his face. The chorus of insects roared to life. He was back in the swamp, every inch of him soaked. He called out for his friend, but only managed to choke up more and more swamp water. Finally, he looked around to see the plane still grounded, firmly wrapped around the tree.

"Jesse!" Cotter's voice cut through the swamp air. But Jesse didn't respond. How many times had they been tricked already? Nothing was real here in this swamp. Not the guidance counselor and not his friend calling out his name. Jesse crawled on his hands and knees through the swamp back towards the bikes, coughing up water with every movement.

Are you faster than your dreams?

The voices echoed from every direction, no longer carried on the wind but rising from the water itself.

It's in the blood.

"Jesse!"

He just had to make it back to the bikes, start his and get as far away from the swamp and forest as possible. He couldn't have gone that far in such a short time. Though he felt guilty, he would leave Cotter here if it meant getting away from the creature.

Jesse stopped, still half submerged in the swamp water. What if this was another dream?

Footsteps. Cotter burst through the underbrush, heading towards him. Was it Cotter? He couldn't be sure anymore. As much as he wanted it to be Cotter, he could be dreaming still.

"Get away from me," he shouted.

The swamp echoed back.

You killed her.

Fear grappled his chest. Jesse picked himself up and sprinted toward the plane. He passed the fuselage, past the torn outside and the blood smeared along the length of the plane. Jesse screamed, but barely louder than the shouts rising all around him.

"What's wrong?"

His mother's eyes, full of life and compassion stared back at him. She smiled and touched his forehead. "You don't look so good, sweetheart."

Jesse threw himself into her arms, feeling the soft brush of her hair against his skin. This time, he couldn't stop the tears from flowing. Tears of relief, joy, confusion, they all began to run down his face.

"I missed you," he said, his face still buried in her shirt. That clean cotton smell filled his nostrils.

"I'm right here," she said. "We're here, together."

He stared into her eyes, looking for any shadow or emptiness. He studied her face for imperfections or blemishes. He ran his hands along her arms, looking for the scars where the razorblade had bit deep into her muscles the night she died. But there were no scars, no gashes, and no trace of her choices. She was as beautiful as the day she took her own life.

"Why are you here?" she asked him.

"I knew you'd be here," Jesse said. He paused for a moment, tears still rolling down his face. "Why did you leave me?" he asked.

She smiled. "I didn't leave you. I'm right here."

"Was I not enough for you?"

Something broke in his mother's face and he knew she was truly gone, that whatever was standing in front of him had no answers.

"I didn't leave you," it said again. "I'm right here."

Jesse sobbed again. "But you did leave me. I needed you, and you left me and Dad."

"I didn't leave you. I'm right here," the voice repeated.

"I always wanted to know why you did it," he said. "But you didn't even know, did you?"

The familiar shadows showed through her eyes, and the once perfect face stretched itself out of proportion once again. Instead of being filled with fear, Jesse found himself wrapped in regret. Though he didn't know why, he felt the same as the night his mother died, filled with questions but never any real answers, especially the ones he needed the most. Any hope for those answers died the night his mother took her own life.

"It's in the blood," it said, smiling through his mother's face.

"I wish you would've chosen me, mom," Jesse said. He hung his head, resigning himself to what he knew was coming next. His mother's face, still smiling, stretched and pulled itself out of proportion as it rose above his head. Her limbs cracked and bent in all directions until she was gone and the only thing standing before Jesse was a towering shadow.

Faced with the thing he feared the most, Jesse put aside his fear and filled himself with sorrow. Sorrow over the life his mother would never know and of the memories that he could never get rid of. He saw his mother, sprawled in her tub, dripping blood across the floor, but there was no life left in her. And he knew she didn't deserve this and neither did he.

"I didn't deserve to lose you," he said.

The creature's knobby fingers curled around his shoulders and pulled him closer.

Seer. It's in the blood.

The long fingers pushed him deeper into the mud and the grime. Jesse choked on the swamp water filling up his lungs. The pain was agonizing, every nerve in his body firing, willing him to act. Maybe this was best though. The thought took hold of him like a dream. If this was the end, maybe it was for the best. After all, it was good enough for his mother. And it would be good enough for him.

He was almost gone, almost to the end, when his body shot up and he began spewing swamp water from his mouth and nostrils. Even amongst the gagging and vomiting, he could hear a voice, shouting with bravado and pomp like only a teenage boy can.

"Get away from my friend, you shithead!" the voice cried.

Jesse pushed himself out of the mud to see Cotter standing over him, waving a handful of leaves, spreading smoke in every direction.

Cotter grabbed Jesse by the shirt and hauled him up to the banks of the swamp, away from the plane and whatever might have lived there. The smell of burning sage drifted along with them, leaving a trail smoke behind them.

Jesse vomited up more water as he rose to his feet. He scampered after Cotter, still blind from the mud, the smell of sage his only clue as to where his friend was leading them. They tore through the underbrush and collapsed next to their bikes.

After a moment of catching his breath, Cotter said, "I don't know what that was, and I don't want to." He tossed the charred sage leaves and pulled a bundle of fresh leaves from his pocket.

Jesse's sight had come back and, though the dark was rising around them, he could finally see the forest clearly. He turned over to see his friend, his chest rising and falling as fast as ever. After a moment, he said, "you saved me."

Cotter laughed. "These things saved you." He held up the sage leaves. "If you hadn't given me these…" he trailed off. "You've got a nasty cut," he said, pointing to Jesse's arm. "Probably from that plane." Cotter found his backpack and produced the whiskey bottle. He opened it and motioned for Jesse to hold out his arm.

The whiskey burned his wound more than it had his throat. Jesse winced as it bubbled and sizzled across his skin. The fumes wafted into the air around them, sending both of their minds buzzing.

"What did you see?" Jesse asked.

Cotter sighed. "I'll tell you now, but I don't ever want to talk about this again," he said. He took a deep breath. Finally, he said, "I saw you run off screaming, then I saw that thing, big ass thing, pushing you down under the water. I don't know what it was, but it wasn't nothing I'd ever seen before. And I don't care to see it again."

There was a long silence between the boys. Cotter poured more whiskey over Jesse's cut. After it was as clean as it could be, Jesse tore a strip from his pants leg and wrapped the cut, his second makeshift bandage of the day.

"Did you see your mom?" Cotter finally asked.

Jesse hesitated. "It wasn't her."

"That sucks," Cotter said.

Jesse stood up and grabbed his dirt bike. He tried the kick starter. The two-stroke engine choked and sputtered, then thumped to life. He couldn't be certain, but he thought he saw a spray of water exit the exhaust. The thought made him shudder again. So he tried to put the swamp out of his mind. He thought, instead, about his cuts and the blood that he had left all throughout the forest. Parts of him would live in this place forever, whether he wanted them to or not. Much like his mother's death, this forest was a part of him now and no matter what answers he did or didn't get, that would never change.

Cotter jumped up, and kick started his own bike. It roared to life in the darkness, and for the first time in a while, both boys felt a spring of hope come over them.

"Thanks," Jesse said.

"For what?"

"For saving me," Jesse said.

Cotter scoffed. "Why wouldn't I?" He mounted his bike and revved the engine. "Besides," he said. "No one deserves to go through all that."

Jesse pulled in the clutch and kicked his bike into gear. "No," he said. "No, they don't."

The tears came again, whether for the loss of his mother or the horrors that he'd made it though, Jesse couldn't be sure. But they were silent this time and welcome, a pleasant release. As the boys raced back towards the edge of the forest, spraying dirt and mud behind them, Jesse let the tears come, drifting down his cheeks and falling to the ground, forever to live somewhere amongst the forest.

www.ingramcontent.com/pod-product-compliance
Lightning Source LLC
LaVergne TN
LVHW051009080826
845145LV00009B/2535

* 9 7 8 1 6 3 8 0 4 2 2 7 3 *